European Sketchbook

European Sketchbook

Brent Stephen Smith

Unless stated otherwise (e.g. excerpts from the author's blog), this is a collection of works of fiction. All names, characters, places, and incidents are a product of the author's imagination. Any resemblance to real events or persons, living or dead, is entirely coincidental.

ISBN: 978-0-9810752-4-2

Brent Stephen Smith
brentstephensmith@gmail.com
brentstephensmith.wordpress.com

"In regards to anything that is within your sphere of influence, I say throw yourself in fullheartedly and dictate life on your terms, living as fully as you choose.

But, in those things which you cannot control, submit yourself with humility and carry yourself with grace."

- June 29, 2011
Ramada Inn, Niedernhausen, Germany
(After missing a connecting flight)

Table of Contents

The Places Inbetween. Or,
Six Nights Without Prose

Budapest. Or. The Sleepy City On The Danube

* * *

Foreword

I feel crazy sometimes. Like, *real*, crazy. I get these urges to jump on the back of a train and just follow it wherever it is going. Living in Canada, the direction the train is going would be pretty apparent. We've got a real West-East thing going on here.

There is a wanderlust itch in me that just keeps needing to be scratched. For whatever reason it also keeps pulling me across the Atlantic.

Whether it is for a high school rugby tour, an academic exchange or a vacation, I just keep ending up over there.

I have been questioned several times about why that is, and I don't have a good answer. I have several plausible responses, but they aren't game-changing answers that will shatter anyone's expectations.

The fact is that I like Europe. The secret is out. I've been blessed to live almost my entire life in Canada, a truly wonderful country in many, many ways. But, I still feel the urge to leave every now and then, and sometimes for long stretches.

Europe is not perfect. I'm not going to argue that. It just happens to have a strange confluence of history, culture and inspiration that keeps calling me.

When given the opportunity to take an extended leave from work and to travel for a few months, inspiration called and I found myself back in Europe, this time mostly in Berlin and Budapest in the late spring/early summer of 2011.

What follows is a selection of what I wrote while there. There are some short stories, blog entries, and excerpts from a beautiful mess of a novel.

I've also included an older short story, "Spanish Air", which was inspired by a previous jaunt through Europe.

None of these pieces can be considered polished, nor should they be. They are selected to show an ephemeral glimpse in time, of that short period when I was just a man with a laptop in a rented room.

-B

Prologue, Or,
That Thing That Comes Before

"Spanish Air"
(May 11, 2009)

The smoke lingered around her mouth before it floated upward into the sticky-warm summer air. A half-drunk pitcher of sangria sat between them, in the open paving-stone plaza. His face betrayed bemusement.

"What?"

He thought how to answer. Staring across from him was a ghost, an ephemeral idea that would illicit fires of gossip back home.

"Nothing, nada."

She took another drag on her cigarette and looked away, disinterested. It was only early June, but the Iberian sun felt scorching to him. Her olive skin and aloofness just seemed to contradict the sweat trickling down his back. He was jealous of the orange slices floating in the pitcher, cooling themselves off.

"It's hot."

She just nodded slightly, lazily watching the tourists walk by, white khaki shorts baring their pink knees.

"We should siesta."

His eyes lit up at the thought. The sangria in his hand remained the only barrier to a midday 'nap'. Not wanting to show too much enthusiasm, *she* never did, he placed the glass on the table.

"Sure, when we've finished our drinks."

A flash of smugness ran through his veins. He had played it cool this time. A minor victory in the thralls of war.

"Okay."

She acquiesced to his small demand. Whether she saw it in the same way as him, he'd never know. It didn't really matter; no, it could not. All of this was a phantom war, a smokescreen to divert attention from more pressing concerns. When all domestic vitals are nearing zero a foreign target needs to be established, something far away, something that is here, but not. A shot in the arm, a reassuring statement that everything is alright, when, most certainly, by all accounts, everything is not alright. Ennui is the symptom, not the cause, pray remember.

"How many times have you gone to the Prado, in your life, would you say?"

"Once."

"Once? That's all?"

"Sí. Just once."

The thought astounded him. Minutes away from where they sat, one of the finest collections of art was housed. She had been once.

"Why only once?"

"I don't know. I've just never felt like going again."

"When did you go?"

"When I was a girl. I went with my school."

"Never again?"

"No."

She put out ash in the tray on the patio table between them. She was neither bothered by, nor interested in, his question. The pitcher was down to a quarter full, perhaps enough for a glass and a half. He filled her unattended glass and topped up his own.

"If I had only two days left here, where would you have me go?"

"What do you mean?"

"If I was leaving in two days, what should I do before I leave?"

"Are you leaving?"

"If, if, *if* I was leaving."

"Well, are you?"

"Maybe, I don't know."

"You don't know?"

"No."

He had caught her attention. They sat in silence, finishing their blood-coloured alcohol. The square around them was emptying itself. The sweaty pink tourists and los Madrileños alike were dispersing to shadier locales. Soon, they too will retire.

"It's hot."

She nodded, this time looking him in the eyes.

"Are you ready?"

"Yes."

They left; a ten-euro bill lay underneath the empty pitcher, walking side-by-side through the plaza. Their hands briefly touched, electricity passing between them. They never held hands; it was too sentimental for her, too reminiscent for him. At unspoken moments in their pasts hand-holding had been commonplace. That was then. Now, under the radiating sun on an early June day, the thought of it withered like a street vendor's unsold fruit.

She turned the key, opened the door, and ushered him in with but a glance. He took his shirt off, fighting it from sticking to his moist back. She opened her apartment's windows and closed the blinds. It was a false privacy with the creaky floors and paper-thin walls surrounding them. There were at least a dozen neighbours in her building at any given moment, perhaps more during the midday heat. If she had any qualms about discretion with him, it had long passed. She had known him for two weeks. They'd made love before. They made love again.

**

"I'm leaving in two days."

"You are?"

"Yes."

"Why?"

"I got an email this morning, well, last night, but I read it this morning from back home."

"Back home."

"I was selected for a summer internship with a top law firm."

"Oh."

She turned on her side and rested her head against his chest. Stupid boy, she thought. Stupid boy for making her see possibility. She had known he would leave sometime; he had to. This was not his place, his space, his home. He was just a stopgap. Someone to fill the seat, for the time being, until another comes along.

"It's a really good job. Good experience before the fall."

He had told her he was going to law school in September. He had just finished his undergrad. The convocation ceremony was next weekend. He would have left Spain in two days, anyways. He couldn't miss that. No, too many would be there, wanting to see his two seconds on stage. The chancellor mispronouncing his name. He walking across the stage, perhaps tripping on the first step up, or down. Sweaty palm shaking hands with the dean who feigns a smile at his graduation. The dean's face red, perhaps a few too many drinks before the ceremony, his own face red, the heat, the attention, blush. The family recording all of this in triplicate.

"So you have to leave?"

"Yes."

He had to. This sojourn was a respite from reality, if only for a few weeks, in between the chaos and banality of middle class scholarship. And yet, he lamented, the European trip was all too clichéd in itself. He steered clear of the touristas and the discotecas they frequented. He eschewed the hostels. When he had first arrived he stayed in a hotel. Why should he care about the cost? Put it on the credit card. That lasted two days. He had not run out of money, or credit, as it were, but had gained the companionship of the raven-haired woman resting her head on him now.

They met at a candy store. She told him he was buying the worst tasting things in the store. "Silly tourist", she playfully scolded him. He asked her to assist him. She obliged. Later that night they found themselves lying in the very same bed. The next day he checked out of the hotel and put his bag in a locker at the train station. "You can't move in with me", she said with a smirk. They spent the next three hundred hours together. Walking, talking, laughing, sitting in silence, the activity didn't matter, for two weeks, they were happy.

"You have gray hairs on your chest."

He was twenty-two. All the stresses in his life were from
the typical experiences of his peers. His graying was
minimal, and notably, only known by a few. There were a
few flecks of gray on his beard, but because he normally
kept himself clean-shaven it was unnoticeable. He hadn't
noticed until he was told it was so. It was in a quiet,
intimate moment like this, a few months prior. Now *she*
had contributed, the words forever to be chiseled in his
head. He stared down at his chest and the admiring
eyes.

"Oh. I do?"

"Yes, just a few."

"So?"

"So, I think it makes you look distinguished."

She giggled dishonestly.

"Clearly, I've planned this all along."

"Before the candy store?"

"Yes."

They spoke as if reading a script from a half-decent
romantic comedy, a charade, too perfect, and surreal.
It was a script for two characters, not them, not "real"
people. As they played in a fantasy world, snippets of
reality drifted in to remind them of the passing grains of
sand that fought against them. Next door they could hear
the barking of a mother, pleading with her children to
behave. It just reminded the two lovers that they would
never be in the same situation, that their love was
crystallized today, but likely to crumble tomorrow.
Their actions were stage directions, mapped out on the
floor, strings attached to their limbs, some unknown
puppeteer awkwardly pulling away. Eventually the final
scene will come, the curtain calls, the audience applauds
and then life erupts again. From the stillness surrounding
the stage during the play rise anxious individuals who

must again return to life. The cars fight the traffic home. The mundane tasks of brushing teeth and hair. Preparing for tomorrow, when once again, they live.

Everything in that bed was a delay to life, and yet, felt so good. Like a vacation that draws close to its end there are contradictory feelings battling throughout the mind and body. It seems reasonable that it would be possible to continue on like this forever, if not for the nagging at the back of the mind. It's pure indulgence; the all-inclusive, and no proper human could live like that for any extended amount of time without being divorced from reality. He felt that. Two weeks of sangria and siesta.

**

In a departure of character she brought him to an Irish pub. It sat next to another Irish pub. They may have been the only two in all of Madrid for how foreign they felt. It might pass as "Little Ireland", an unofficial embassy, or a beacon for Anglophones. Inside the bar they could hear nothing but outsiders. Kiwis, Scots, Aussies, Americans, English, Canadians, even Polish voices reverberated. She had left her comfort zone as a small concession, perhaps a last desperate attempt to reconcile the divergence between his life and hers. She ordered a Guinness, bewildering him in the process. On the television screens played highlights of North American sports.

"Pau Gasol scored 18 points."

"Oh."

He glanced around and all he saw were pink-skinned tourists. And her. The dim pub lighting revealed bags under her eyes he had not noticed before. The dark, frothy pint glass seemed wrong in her hands. Everything

just seemed off. It was as if the actors had been left
without a script, or set, and their ability to improvise was
rigid and awkward, forced.

"I'll be right back."

Entering the WC he stared directly into the mirror and
saw for the first time what he had omitted to admit
everyday since he had arrived: he was nothing more
than a pink-skinned tourist. Two weeks playing native
hadn't changed that. The blood rushed to his face,
highlighting his pinkness.

All of this had been wrong. It was so awkward. He felt
the strings of his heart being pulled, perhaps by the
puppeteer, more likely his conscience. How could he
have fallen in love with her? It was fleeting; it would
never last, right? He was leaving Madrid in two days.
Did he want to spend it perpetuating a fantasy? Was it a
fantasy? Best to make the most of it, if it was.

He left the washroom and returned to find an empty table
with two pints of the black stuff unattended. Underneath
her glass, written in lipstick, was a napkin note:

"lo siento"

**

"Open the door."

"Who is this?"

"You know who it is. Open the door."

"I'm sorry. My English bad. Goodbye."

"Please. I have to speak with you."

She said nothing more. What could she say?

He slumped down against the wall, outside her door, waiting. What was this? He had spent two weeks playing make-believe with a beautiful Castilian woman, trying to escape the real world that waited for him on the other side of the Atlantic. Only now, did he realise, the real world did not stop, but followed him wherever he went. I love her, he thought. Three feet away, worlds apart, his heart broke for her.

**

He stands in line, waiting to hear his name called, his cue to walk across the stage. His family sits in the crowd, broad smiles across their face. The auditorium is sweltering. A little sweat bead works its way down his father's forehead, swatted away by a tissue. His mother is frantically trying to figure out the video feature on the digital camera. He hears his name, slightly stumbles going up the stairs to the stage, and receives his degree.

"Congratulations."

"Gracías."

He takes the walk across the stage, hears the applause, and waves coyly. Dismounting from the stage he walks to his parents, hands them the envelope and leaves.

**

"Open the door."

Berlin, Or,
The Sexy City On The Spree

"Notes from the Underslept"
(Blog entry. April 28. 2011)

The rain comes down with a loud, awful din. I'm watching the baggage crew outside hustle and shimmy around the tarmac. At the departure gate, inside, it's warm and (of course) dry, and I'm thankful I'm not one of them out there. I sip my last Canadian coffee (a large double-double from the ubiquitous giant) and slouch down in my seat. I've found one of the few sofa-style chairs. Unlike the standard row upon row chairs that thousands find themselves uncomfortably upright in, my chair is welcoming. I slouch way back until I can imagine every medical practitioner I've ever met frowning. So relaxed.

And nervous. The weight of the enormity of it all hits me in successive waves. I'm excited and ecstatic for the possibilities ("Oh Possibility!") and adventures I will surely find myself in. I'm terrified that I'm going it alone, and, despite the fact that I am "blessed" with being a native speaker of English, the world's second language, I'm worried about having to interact with a very large number of people in several other firsts. The thoughts of this only begin to hit when I overhear the other passengers waiting for our flight. There is a lot of German being spoken. I don't understand a word of it, and am shamefully inadequate in even being able to apologise for not speaking it. How often could that come up?

I get up and decide to stretch my legs and go for a walk. It's going to be a long flight, after-all. Eyeing the woman who had perched herself atop the end of the nearest row, I knew my sofa would be gone when I return. Having no comfortable home to return, I walk the length of the terminal. It's not far. In a sort of casual nervousness, most passengers sit tapping their fingers or checking their watches, re-reading their tickets (heaven forbids all those steps leading to this moment when someone checked your ticket and looked you over was for not), jumping up and having to go piddle ("watch my bags, will you?"), pretending not to watch the many LCD screens plastered throughout ("Royal Wedding Update 2,895,143,659: Wills to wear a tuxedo!") and cagily planning the quickest route to jam themselves at the boarding gate when it's time to go (the answer is a banal "walk straight into wherever the existing line crosses your own path and 'pretend' like you don't notice the person you've intersected"). Yes, most everyone is doing and thinking the exact same thing.

Well, almost everyone. There's a certain group of parents who've decided that their authority does not, in fact, stretch past the x-ray and body scanner machines of security. It's hard to argue with their logic. After having watched Mommy and Daddy have to take off and temporarily discard any semblance of what it means to be an adult (watches, belts, mobile phones, etc.), it's not hard for little Ethan, or Evan, or Emmanuel to recognise that absolutes are not absolute. When little Judith, or Julie, or Jasmine refuses to behave a certain way, the "because I'm your [insert parental figure of choice]" loses much of its meaning, when that [parental figure] just got groped by the security agent, like a common suspect. Nonetheless, after having their Emperor's Clothes revealed, these parents have caved. Anything past security, from the over-priced café stand to the three inches of space next to my ear have been given to the Ritalin runts to do as they please. Financial Post Papa and Blackberry Mama will only occasionally call out to come sit down.

**

I wake up in a haze. I have no idea what time it is. I have no idea what time zone I'm in. Time is, for all intents and purposes, meaningless. There is the world Out There, where normal, linear understandings of time (sun, moon, days, hours, etc.) apply. Then there is the world In Here. In Here, I have no idea what is going on. We were served dinner, I think, just a few hours (?) ago, possibly yesterday (?). I want to say I had the chicken. Just to be safe, I always order the chicken (like an *Inception* totem). I feel like I've slept for hours. I check my iPhone (obviously set to Airplane Mode – when time need not apply). The numbers just don't make sense. It's only 11pm (in Ottawa?). Maybe. I really don't know. Accounting for dinner (likely chicken), the movie I watched (*Dinner for Schmucks* [2010]), and the last song I remember listening to compared to where my playlist now sits, I'd say I may have slept for thirteen minutes. How is that possible? What Time Lord has messed with me? Get me out of this damned Tardis! I watch *True Grit* to the end, turn on some more music, and fall asleep again.

**

Someone opens the window shade three rows ahead and a blast of sunshine comes into the cabin. I remember how forcefully the flight attendant had come around earlier and slammed the shades down. I almost expect her to return and punish the day-bringer. Nothing happens. In Here, under Sky Law, the rules are made up on the spot and enforced with a haphazard inconsistency. Women are sent at one moment to the back of the plane to urinate, and the next, the middle of the plane. Pandemonium! I choose to sit quietly at my window seat and wait until others have opened their shades before I boldly affront the rules of the Sky.

On the screen in front of me, in what is meant to be informative, a countdown of sorts scrawls across the screen. Miles Travelled. Miles to Destination. Time of Arrival. Minutes to Arrival. Seemingly helpful information, but I can't make sense of it. The screen flashes to a different view, a different angle. Our flight path is animated as an orange arrow over a blank blue background. Now we're charting over a topographic map of the Atlantic. It's filled with detailed demarcations of all the different underwater peaks and valleys. Now a world map, with time zones. Now a world map with a parabolic

arch marking the division between night and day. Where
are we? Now a close up map of us, over underwater
ridges I had never heard of before, nor cared to learn.
More Miles Travelled. Fewer Miles to Destination.
Our Time of Arrival is now three minutes earlier. Now it is
four minutes later. Is that our original arrival time?
How is there still three hours to go until arrival?
What day is this? So, so, so very confused. I make a
vow never to take another Red Eye in my life.
After glancing at other people's screens I also vow never
to watch *Little Fockers*.

All the cabin lights come on. Sky Law no longer cares
about our puny window shades. Coffee comes. Also, a
"muffin" ("Rectangular loaves can never be muffins, Sky
Mistress"). We're over Belgium. Thank goodness for
that. That's far easier for me to imagine than the abstract
geography I was treated to earlier.

**

It's 9am in Frankfurt. Of that, I am sure. My body
disagrees. And so do the travellers in the airport café
line in front of me. They've all ordered beers. I'm
certainly not a teetotaller, but 9am on a Thursday (?) at
an airport isn't really my time to grab a pint. When I buy
my "kaffee", I can see that the canny travellers had gone
with beer because it was cheap. My coffee, though, I'll
admit, it is organic ("bio-kaffee"), came in at 4 euros, or
almost six dollars Canadian. In contrast, those lovely
lushes are drinking 500ml of morning goodness for 2.50
euros. Oh, and did I mention it's draught beer. None of
that bottled stuff. I feel like a sucker.

I retreat with my bio-kaffee to wait by the gate for my
connecting flight to Berlin. After being bombarded with
one million arrows pointing one million directions in sans
serif font over primary colour blocks, I could use a
retreat. Intensity is not necessarily my thing in the
morning, let alone during a long journey. After winding
through hallway after hallway, with moving walkways,
golf carts, bicycles, and on at least one occasion

a carry-on suitcase-scooter hybrid [Note: I later found said item in the Lufthansa World Shop catalogue onboard, if you're interested], I was finding it hard not to believe that I was actually in an airport and not the centre of a major metropolis. Everything I had seen before in my life no longer mattered. This was it. This is the 21st Century, folks. This is what we've all been progressing towards. From the Classical era of Aristotle, to Locke's Enlightenment, nothing could be more magnificent of human achievement than the continental hub of Frankfurt International, with special mention to the waves of yellow and blue Lufthansa logos, podiums, kiosks, carts, and personnel, that just reinforced the feeling that business was business and business is good. I should have been thanking the stars that every action in my life had led to this moment, sipping bio-kaffee in humanity's zenith.

I'm not. I am crammed at the edge of a bench (yes, those row by row ones) surrounded by a swarm of elderly tourists, clucking away in an indiscriminate Pan-European language that seems to encapsulate every Slavic, Latin and Germanic word. They are presumably travelling as a group (or are very familiar with strangers) and have made it their mission to set up camp on every square centimetre of surface at Gate 21. The men all seem to be wearing red sweaters with plaid collared shirts underneath. I can only see space disappearing and where it once existed now rests plaid collared shirts smartly matched with a light red sweater. I no longer have a table to rest my bio-kaffee on, as one Pan-Euro woman swooped in and made it a seat (they lack not for invention). No matter, that only causes a fuss with the gentleman who had reached behind me to grab a newspaper. The two of them cluck away. The man gets his paper. The table woman has moved on to terrorize the German woman sat across from me that very clearly has flight anxiety. Her husband had been doting to her every need and her nerves seem frayed to the point of meltdown. Her husband leaves and she optimistically places her purse on his seat to guard it. Within seconds another Pan-European Elder claims the spot next to it.

A friend arrives and inquires about the vacant spot
where the purse rests. The nervous German tells them
off in a very universal way. I can't blame her. Between
the flight anxiety and the hive of locusts (yeah, why
not?), this woman really ought not to have to worry about
a seat. I, for one, subscribe to the philosophy that I'd
rather lose a friendship than save a seat (no, friends,
I will not save a row of seats at the cinema for you to
show up at the last minute on cheap Tuesdays).
Who needs the stress?

The boarding commences and a new level of European
sophistication emerges. I shouldn't have doubted that
Frankfurt International, evolutionary peak of international
travel, would rise to the occasion. In a charmingly
simplistic move, Lufthansa has adopted the same
procedure as getting on a metro to getting on an
airplane. Ah yes! Public transportation has always been
a feather in the cap for Europe and why not apply that
same model to the sky? As soon as boarding is
announced, scores of people push and clamour to get to
the gates, which are nothing more than futuristic
turnstiles. Scan ticket. Gate opens. Next person. But, like
rush hour commuters hoping not to miss the train, three
or four people are trying to scan their tickets, while
shuffling their bodies towards the plane (I should also
mention, we have assigned seats). Amazingly (to me, at
least – frequenter of segregated loading of planes:
priority, first class, back of plane, middle of plane, etc.),
it works. Except for the one guy who decides that twenty
centimetres from the gate he better make that phone
call. I have heard hecklers before, but nothing like the
torrent of multi-lingual abuse that fellow heard. And then,
as soon as it came, it's over; we're on the plane, seated
and ready to go.

**

The carousel stops turning. A confused look crosses the
faces of the forty or so of us that are still waiting for our
checked luggage. The screen above the carousel says
in German and English that baggage delivery is finished.

Next thing I see, most of the people waiting are gone. The Pan-European Elderly Locusts of the Futuristic Departures Gate, travelling as a bus tour, apparently, were given word (presumably in whatever Pan-European hybrid language they spoke) where to go and they are gone. It is left to the remaining half-dozen of us to ask questions and wander through the thankfully "quaint" Berlin-Tegel airport to find the lost luggage office.

There, in a reversal of the frenetic optimism of Frankfurt, we all wait silently. Even the clucking of the Pan-Europeans has stopped. Next to the office is a currency exchange and I spot a 20 euro bill sitting on a lower part of the customer's side of the counter. No customer remains, and I see the agent walk away from the counter. I walk over, pick up the bill and stand staring at the plexiglass divider. The agent comes and asks me what I'd like. I tell him in simple English that this bill was left by the last customer. I don't know if he'll come back, but if he does, here it is. The agent looks confused and takes the bill. I rejoin the line for the lost luggage. I don't really think too much about that bill, though a small, non-rational part of my brain hopes that a bit of karmic help might come along.

I talk to the lost baggage agent and she takes my contact information. They have no idea what happened to the bags, but they didn't come from Frankfurt with us. Hopefully they were even in Frankfurt. Travelling from Canada, I fear my bag might be any parts in between (perhaps at the bottom of one of those unknown topographical sea valleys). I'm given a tracking number and, as a gift, a men's overnight bag as an apology.

As it stands, I'm missing my checked backpack with all my clothes for two months, some books, and a few bathroom necessities (which the Apology Bag helps cover). With me, thankfully, is every single valuable, which I had carried on me and my carry-on. I have all my reservation information, cash, meds, glasses, laptop, camera, etc.

I make it to the rented flat with no problem (one-way single ticket zone AB), and catch some shut-eye; regardless of the fact that I'm told it's the afternoon. I'll figure out this linear time business later, once I return to the world Out There.

"Tilly the Bear's Intervention"
(April 29, 2011)

Tilly the Bear sat in his country cottage, engorging himself on maple syrup. He thought nothing wrong with that. Really, the thought of a bear owning a cottage did not seem the least bit preposterous. Also, this bear, Tilly, happens to have an eating disorder. He calls it a sweet tooth, but his friends and family are concerned, nonetheless. So he sat there, in the country cottage, at a handcrafted wooden table and in a chair, or a stool, if that would be quainter. I don't know where Tilly got the handcrafted wooden kitchen suite, but I suppose a bear could really get anything he put his mind to if he wanted it. What carpenter would disagree with him? Tilly emptied the jar of syrup into his fat sticky mouth and tossed it in the corner with the other ones. It was a Friday, and on Fridays, Tilly got his binge on.

A light rapping at the door disturbed Tilly from opening up another jar of maple syrup. I would normally pity the stupid fool who would get between a ravenous grizzly and his meal, but the fellow at the door was welcomed in by Tilly. Of course, the guest happened to be a pint-sized pig called Runt. That's just how these names come about. Also, would you believe a pig could be called Reginald? Miraculously enough, though less so if you are starting to sense a pattern here, the pig started to speak. In words. English words. He's a pig.

"G-g-g-g-good evening, Tilly."

He may speak, but Runt has the burden of a speech impediment.

"Hello, Runt. How are you?"

Tilly has the most boring voice one could imagine. It's hard to tell if it's natural (what with him being a bear and

all) or if it is the result of riding high on syrup for weeks
on end.

"F-f-f-fine, Tilly. Thanks."

Tilly, as a host, realizes he ought to offer something to
his guest. He may be a bear riddled with addiction, but
that doesn't mean he lacks manners.

"Can I get you something?"

Surveying the piles of empty maple syrup jars, Runt
heeds to caution.

"C-c-c-can I have some t-t-t-t-tea?"

Relieved that the pig didn't want to devour any of his
syrup, Tilly hops up and starts rummaging through the
cupboards. Clouds of dust fill the air and Runt knows
that his friend hasn't been consuming anything by syrup
for a very long time.

"O-o-o-oh dear."

"Don't worry about it, Runt. I got this. I swear there's
some tea in here, somewhere."

Tilly throws his paws around in a manic fit, searching for
that box of tea he swears is in there, somewhere.

"Here it is."

A stale old box of Earl Grey sits on the table in front of
Runt.

"G-g-goodness."

"Let me grab the kettle."

Tilly creates another whirlwind of dust before emerging
with a teakettle.

"There we go, Runt. Should be ready in just a second. Excuse me while I go down to the cellar and grab some syrup for myself."

"O-o-of course."

With Tilly out of the room, Runt takes the opportunity to call his friends.

"Y-y-y-you need to get down here. T-t-t-tilly is out of control. He's on a b-b-b-b-bender."

Runt hangs up and helps himself to the kettle, pouring the hot water into his cup.

"Ah good, Runt, you put yourself to work."

"Y-y-yes. No problem."

"Well, now that your tea is ready, let's have a toast, shall we?"

"O-o-o-okay."

Tilly holds up a fresh jar of syrup and looks his porcine friend in the eyes.

"To my best friend in the whole world, Runt."

"Ch-ch-cheers."

Runt nervously sips his tea. Cracking twigs on the walkway catch Tilly's ears.

"Did you hear that, Runt?"

"N-n-n-n-no."

Tilly goes to the window and pulls the shade aside briefly, looking out.

"I think there is someone out there."

"R-r-r-really?"

"I hate it when people come unannounced!"

Tilly rushes to the back of the cottage, knocking over some of his empty syrup jars.

"I'm going to see what's up out there."

Tilly is wearing a sweater. I don't know why.

"M-m-m-maybe just wait, Tilly."

Tilly turns his big old bear face at the little pig.

"Why?"

A lump passes down Runt's throat as he realizes that maple syrup is a delicious addition to bacon.

"M-m-m-maybe it's people we know."

Tilly scowls, only in a bearlike way.

"I hope so."

There is a knock at the door. Tilly looks out the window to see his circle of friends and some minor acquaintances.

"Drats."

Tilly opens the door.

"What are you all doing here?"

An old hare, appropriately called Old Harry answers for the group.

"We're worried about you, Tilly."

"What?"

A depressed donkey called Marcel clears the air.

"This is an intervention, Tilly. You have a problem."

"That's rich coming from you, Marcel. You're suicidal!"

Tilly slams the door in their faces. He turns to Runt.

"And you! You had something to do with this, didn't you?"

"L-l-l-l-listen, l-l-l-l-let me explain m-m-m-m-myself."

"Listen? Are you out of your mind, Runt? I don't have time to listen to you. That would take forever. Get out of my house!"

Fearing for his life, Runt abides.

"S-s-s-sorry, Tilly."

Outside, on Tilly's front lawn the group tries to discuss what their plan of action is.

"I think Tilly will listen to Walla, she's a parental figure, after all."

The short stocky female wallaby looks at the group.

"I'd rather we just stop being friends with Tilly. He's a bad influence on Bea."

She looks down at the sleeping toddler in her pouch, inexplicably wearing pyjamas.

"Come on, Walla, you can't mean that."

"I do mean it. In fact, I think most of you are rather awful role models."

Runt looks hurt.

"Even me, Walla?"

"Yes, definitely. I don't agree with… I don't agree with your, let's call it 'lifestyle', Runt."

"Oh."

Old Harry, the old hare, intervened.

"Now, now, let's not aggravate this."

"And you, Harry, you really ought not to speak. We've all heard about the rumours about your past."

"That was a long time ago!"

"It's not an excuse for what happened, Harry."

"I paid my dues! I did my time."

"You disgust me, and if you ask everyone else what they say about you behind your back, you'd know that you disgust them, too."

Old Harry turned his eyes towards the others and each one of them just looked away.

"I just want to be left alone to tend to my garden."

Jumping out of the bushes came Pander, the panther.

"Easy, Pander! You scared us all."

"No worries, no worries, no worries! Pander is just here to have fun!"

Pander just continues bounding about. Runt turns to Marcel.

"Who invited Pander?"

"I believe that Harry did."

Walla tries to grab Pander and speak to him, but he bounces away from her.

"Pander is even a better bouncer than you, Walla!"

"You are not meant to bounce, Pander. You are a panther."

Pander stops and looks the marsupial seriously in the eyes.

"And what, pray tell, does being a panther entail?"

Walla says nothing. Pander returns to his bouncing.

"We must figure out a way to wean Tilly off his syrup addiction."

"He seems fine to Pander!"

"Oh great, the addict seems fine to the hyperactive transpecies."

"May I say something?"

"Yeah, why not, Harry? Why not let you have your say? Hey, Runt, Pander, Marcel, come and listen to what Old Harry wants to say."

Old Harry mumbles something to himself and then speaks to the group.

"I'll be the first to admit that I've made mistakes."

He looks Walla in the eyes and then continues.

"But, after paying the penance for those mistakes, and changing my life, I can honestly say that I am much happier with the life that I have. Shouldn't we wish to help Tilly, so he can live the life he was meant to have."

"I-I-I-I for one agree."

"You would, Runt. You already are living the life you want for Tilly."

"W-w-w-w-what do you mean?"

"Just admit it, you are in love with Tilly."

"I-I-I-I-I admit that we are good friends."

"As good of friends as you and I?"

"W-w-w-w-well, Walla, it's complicated, see."

"Because I am a woman?"

"N-n-n-n-n-no, of course not. Mostly because you are a wallaby. A-a-a-a-a-also aren't you a n-n-n-n-new mother. H-h-h-h-h-how long after you got pregnant b-b-b-b-before Bea's father split?"

"How dare you, you little runt. I'd rock your world."

Just then her toddler woke up.

"What's going on, Mama?"

"Back to sleep, Bea!"

She closes the top of her pouch with a zipper.

"That's better. Now listen here, I said this last week at Marcel's intervention and I'll say it again. This group can't get much more dysfunctional. I don't know why I bother to stay around with you all. I really don't. There is no explanation."

"Well, Walla, there could be one reason."

"Not now, Marcel!"

Everyone looks at the donkey.

"Walla and I have been together for a while, on and off again."

"Quiet, Marcel!"

"R-r-r-r-really?"

Walla looks at Marcel and then at the rest of the group.

"Maybe."

Tilly's front door opens.

"What are you all still doing here? Get lost!"

"Hey Tilly! How's it going? Wanna bounce?"

"Not right now, Pander."

"T-t-t-tilly, there is something I need to say."

"Go home, Runt."

"O-o-o-okay."

"Would you just consider the ramifications of your actions, Tilly?"

"That hurts coming from you, Harry. At least my actions don't harm others."

"Self-inflicted pain can cause ripples through the group and create psychological discord for the rest of us."

"Don't quote me, Marcel. I said that last week at your intervention!"

"Sorry, Tilly."

The group begins to walk away from Tilly's cottage. Walla lingers behind.

"Do you want to come in, Walla?"

"Sure, it's getting cold out."

"Can I make you some tea? I discovered I have some Earl Grey."

"You know I don't want tea."

"Not this again, Walla. I won't have it."

"I just want you to spend some time with Bea, that's all."

"Give it a rest, Walla, we know she's not mine."

"We don't know that."

"I checked with Owen the Owl and he seems to think it's biologically impossible."

"What? You went to Owen without me?"

"I needed a wise mind to crack that puzzle. You can't blame me, can you?"

"I just thought you'd take me at my word."

"Listen, Walla, it just made sense to me, I think you can understand that when a bear is in the middle of a maple syrup binge and he's at an interspecies orgy he has the right to know if a child is his."

"I wanted it to be yours."

"Yes, well wanting is not enough."

"No?"

"No, it's not. There just isn't enough wanting in the world to make it so."

"I'm sorry, Tilly."

"It's okay, Walla, I can't blame you. It must be hard for you living in an ecosystem that isn't yours. It's bound to make a wallaby do some crazy things."

"Yes, I've certainly done a few."

"I'll say."

Tilly took Walla's paws in his own and looked her in the eyes.

"If I ever hear that you and Marcel sleep together again, so help me, I will eat you."

Excerpt from

"So Schmeckt Berlin: Adventures in Flavourful Berlin"
(Blog entry, April 30, 2011)

I began to discover my neighbourhood a bit. I'm staying in an area called Wedding, in the Northwest part of central Berlin. It's mostly a fairly quiet, residential area. There is a major S-Bahn station that is just a short walk away along the one major street I've seen in the area, though it is hardly worth mentioning. There are a couple bank branches and, of course, the "sight" of the area, the Bayer pharmaceuticals complex. Tucked aside from the busy roads are a lot of smaller streets, all with medium-sized apartment blocks (five or so floors) and small businesses (art galleries, convenience stores, bakeries, etc.) below.

Despite the presence of Bayer, there are a lot of small parks and the overall feeling of Wedding is one of Industrial Naturalism or Natural Industrialism (still not sure how to define it). It seems to be pretty common throughout Berlin, that it is a real working-class city, with factories and smokestacks mixed with plenty of greenery. That being said, there also seems to be a good mix of people and they seem to run in different circles. Berlin really is a crazy, heterogeneous, muesli of people, things and ideas.

Heading south on foot from my apartment I run into the Spree, the river that dissects the city. The next neighbourhood, Tiergarten, begins here. When the weather is good (and it's been mostly good), people gather on the spots of sand or stretches of grass and bask in the sun, sing songs and of course, drink a beer. For the more adventurous, inflatable tubes make for good travelling, keeping in mind that not that much further down the river one runs into the tour boats.

I later saw one woman inflating a raft Saturday afternoon when I was walking to the supermarket. She had oars and everything. I wish I had asked her where she planned to go.

A pathway runs parallel to the Spree and so do I, discovering that it just twists and turns with the river and incorporates the local architecture, as well. A part of the path actually goes underneath a modernist condo building, while another gets slightly diverted from the river to jut through a cemetery. Keep heading south, be patient with a few pedestrian crossings, and find yourself at the gorgeous glass Hauptbahnhof, a relatively new central rail station. It was built for the World Cup in 2006, and apparently opened up just in time. I wouldn't have even known.

Back in May 2006, the last time I was in Berlin, just one week before the World Cup commenced, I was still arriving by train at one of the older stations. Despicable! There will be none of that this time. I'm going all out. I can already look forward to departing in a high-speed train from there in two weeks for Hamburg, when I go to see the Manic Street Preachers concert.

Further past the Hauptbahnhof is the centre of German government, the Reichstag. It is a beautiful building, a mixture of stone and glass. I'm planning to go and take a tour sometime in the next few weeks that I am here, but one look at the line to get in makes me think that I'll cross a few other things off my list first.

Exhausted and sweating in the late spring sun, I do a light stretch in the shade of a bridge, turn around and run back to Wedding. I don't know if it's the run, by I couldn't imagine all those suckers standing in line sweltering in the heat. At least at the Brandenburger Tor (Brandenburg Gate) you can sit down and have a pint.

**

Now, for what most of you must be wondering: what of the tastes of Berlin? Good question (I'll assume that you did ask that). Having only spent a few days here, I've only had a few local delicacies (or variations of the familiar). Early on, though, I made a decision that I would eschew chewing anything from a North American fast food joint. There is only so much McDonald's and Burger King that a man can eat, and I think that at 26, I have reached that point. But, I can't rule out the local stuff that is bad for you, otherwise where's the fun?

On Thursday night, after collapsing to sleep from exhaustion, I woke and went for a late night wander down my street. Remembering that "imbiss" is basically the word for crap food, I check out a local Turkish shop, for their version of a doner kebab. Unfortunately, luck had either run out for me, or intervened (given recent stomach bouts with shwarma), and the spinning doner meat skewer was empty. With a little assistance from an English-speaking customer, before he had to leave, I ended up with a breaded chicken kebab sandwich, slathered in three different sauces ("I don't know what you're saying, so let's have everything, bitte."). Looking at the menu, I also saw that they served beer (which was the revelation that in Germany, everyone sells beer). I order a familiar bottle of Beck's (500ml for 1.20 euros). Overall, it was not a bad first official meal in Germany. The chicken sandwich was a bit like I expected it to be: it felt thrown together out of necessity rather than design. As for the Beck's, it was a pleasurable beverage for someone who didn't know about too many German beers.

Over the course of the past few days, I've been trying my luck at new beers, and buying them at wherever I might find them. As one might imagine, despite the fact that everyone sells beer, there is a sharp price gradation throughout the city, depending on both geography and type of vendor (and thirdly, beer brand).

Obviously, as one might imagine, the "express" stand at Brandenburger Tor where I bought an Erdinger Weissbier was expensive (3.20 euros). At Netto, a discount store, where I bought a Sternburg Export, it was very cheap (0.38 euros). A fairly standard price at a grocer, like Kaiser's is around 0.70 euros for a 500ml bottle of a mainstream brand (Erdinger, Berliner Kindl, Schultheiss, Beck's, etc.). At a convenience store or a kebab shop those same beers are around 1 euro each. I haven't ordered beers at a proper restaurant yet (nor eaten there), but based on the chalkboards outside we're looking at "express" stand at the Brandenburger Tor price range. I can't imagine what a club would charge. All that being said, the 0.38 euro bottle of Sternburg was definitely passable.

To really describe the cheapest of the cheap though, is something else. On Saturday, in an Aldi (another discount supermarket), I found a 6-pack of 500ml PLASTIC bottles for 1.69 euros, total. I can't remember the name of the brand, but it was unfamiliar, and after drinking pints from glass bottles at the foot of the Brandenburg Gate, you can bet I thought twice about buying a 6-pack of plastic discount beers.
Maybe another day. In any case, I had filled my bag with useless food to get me through the weekend and had no room for plastic beer.

But enough about beer (for now), the one thing I had heard before about Berlin's food was to try the currywurst. I had been holding out for a couple of days until I could make it down to Kreuzberg and try one of the highly acclaimed currywurst stands (it seems silly as I type it). However, under the heat of Saturday's afternoon sun, after strolling from Alexanderplatz, past the Berliner Dom, down Unter den Linden, and to the foot of the Gate, I was famished. I mentioned the Erdinger Weissbier, but I didn't mention what it had to wash down. The currywurst is a really simple, though intriguing snack. The local sausage is cut into chunks and then drowned in a spicy ketchup-like sauce and sprinkled with curry powder, served on a paper plate.

You're given a tiny plastic fork (or a toothpick depending on the stand) and a bread roll and told to have at it. It was pretty good. I'm still going to have to head out to Kreuzberg and stand in line at the critically acclaimed Curry 36 stand (yes, I will stand in line for currywurst before I stand in line at the Reichstag).

"Ugly Logic"
(May 1, 2011)

"You can't be serious!"

Patti was unconvinced with Petr's argument.

"I am. I truly am serious, Patricia. You must believe me."

"I just can't. Is that wrong? Am I wrong, everyone?"

The group looked at Patti and just burst out in laughter. Uli, a young man, no older than twenty-three, spoke.

"What do you find so objectionable about Petr's thesis, Patti?"

Patti looked at Uli and imagined him as her younger brother, smugly returned from university on a break, spouting of his newfound love of buckwheat and Balkan yoghurt.

"I find the majority of it objectionable, Uli. That is the first problem. I don't wish to pick away at small details, but it certainly is offensive, to me."

"But which parts? Do entertain us."

"Fine, for the sake of starting an argument, let's agree that it is morally acceptable for a man to steal a loaf of bread to feed his children."

The group murmured in agreement.

"Right, so that is settled, then. We can agree that on the whole, while theft is generally considered unpleasant and unwanted in a civilised society, it may, due to extenuating circumstances, come to be seen as acceptable out of a greater moral imperative, in this case the extension of the poor man's children's lives."

The group murmured again in agreement with Patti.

"But, I made the mistake of asking how many times the man might have to steal."

Uli began to speak but let Patti continue.

"We all agreed at that point, that it may come to pass that the poor man might have to steal many times for his starving children, at which point the one act of sin is now magnified into many acts. I asked if we thought that would still be okay. As a group we all agreed that it might be necessary, though we were less certain at this point than before when it was a question of a single act of theft."

Petr poured more wine in Patti's glass and watched his girlfriend speak.

"Thank you, Pet. So, we now came to the argument that perhaps it might be necessary to steal more to provide for his starving kids. But we could not agree on what was acceptable. Lisa, John, and Marcia thought that it was entirely fine for the poor man to steal as much food as his kids needed to survive. Mark, Lee-Anne, and Sally thought that if the kids needed warm clothes or a blanket that too would be acceptable. I merely asked what our thoughts would be if we were the fruit seller, or the baker, or the clothes merchant. Mark and Sally thought that so long as the poor man did not steal from the same people all the time it might mitigate the costs, both morally and materially. Uli stated that he thought that the poor man might be able to time his thefts so as to acquire food that was nearly spoilt, so as to not upset the grocer. We disagreed upon whether it was better for the man to feed his children spoiled food or let them starve. It was around this time that Petr, the love of my life, suggested that if the poor man was to steal so much so as to affect the livelihood's of the community, it might be morally imperative of him to do the act which would have the smallest impact."

Uli spoke again.

"Yes, Patti. That seems like a rational proposal, no?"

"But tell me, Uli, what act could a poor man, an outcast in a society perpetrate that would have the smallest impact on a community while ultimately solving once and for all the problem of the starving children?"

"I don't know. I didn't really see it out. What do you think that means?"

"I think I know exactly what it means and it bothers me that my boyfriend would suggest it."

"What is it, Petr?"

"The man ought to kill his children."

The group looked shocked and in awe of the very revolting idea. What had begun, as an interesting exercise of their minds, had turned very dark, very quickly. They looked at Petr calmly drinking his pinot noir and wondered how he could look so calm.

"That is infanticide, Petr!"

"You're right, Mark. It is."

"That's horrible!"

"It is. But, if you all remember this was supposed to be a solution for an ongoing problem. If the poor man had no other means to support his children than to steal from the town, affecting their livelihoods and showed no possible way of correcting the issue of their destitution, what kind of live could he possibly offer them?"

"Well done, Petr. You've at least shown them why I was so bothered by the thought."

"It was just a rational solution to a problem."

"It troubles me that your mind considers that rational."

"It was a way to minimize the impact of the problem."

"By destroying human lives?"

"What about all the lives that man might destroy because of his thievery? What if his stealing causes the grocer to go broke and his family is out on the streets, too?"

"That does make a good point, Patti."

"I for one, think that if the man was to spread his stealing evenly no single family would suffer enough to notice and he might still be able to support his children."

"That's a nice idea, Mark, but the problem with that is for how long? Does he steal for five years, ten, twenty? Why not have the community just give the stealing man financial support?"

"Yes, in a way it's the same idea."

"So they can steal from the left hand instead of the right."

"Uli, you can't mean that."

"Sure, what's the difference between having a man come in your back window and steal a loaf of bread once a week for his entire life or to have your income taxed to give the same man the money to buy a loaf of bread?"

"Uli has a good point."

"Lee-Anne! I would never imagine you thinking that!"

"Well, it's true, though, isn't it?"

"In a way, I suppose."

Sally, silent for most of the debate finally spoke up.

"So, if I follow Petr's suggestion that the action with the smallest overall impact ought to be the course taken, and, if I accept Uli's assertion that stealing from the community as a whole is just as bad as providing financial support, the logical conclusion is that we ought to kill all people on social supports?"

"I never said that."

"I certainly wouldn't agree to that."

"But that's basically a logical conclusion, right Petr?"

Petr's face was red. Patti was beaming with pride in her friend.

"No, Sally, I don't think so."

"Because, in essence, we could all argue that regardless of what kind of financial support a society provides the origin of that support, income taxation, affects families the same. It is the same as stealing a loaf of bread once per week for life, right Uli?"

"Well, uh, I don't know if it's that simple."

"I agree, Sally. We might even agree that if it affects the payers equally, priority ought to be given to the recipients most in need."

"Excellent point, Patti."

The two girls lit up at this point.

"Mark, who do you think deserves the equivalent of a loaf of bread per week more, the starving man and his children, or a university student?"

"The starving man and his children."

"John, who do you think deserves the equivalent of a loaf of bread per week more, the starving man and his children, or an independent film maker?"

John sighs.

"The starving man and his children."

"Uli, how many loaves of bread could you have bought instead of that bottle of pinot?"

"Well, it depends on the type of bread."

"Imagine you're starving. You're buying the cheapest, biggest loaves you can."

"Probably about fifteen or twenty."

Patti smiles at the young man.

"It was a very delicious red, though, I will admit."

Petr looked at his girlfriend and felt a mixture of pride and disagreement.

"So, what, Patti? So, what of it all? You can't fault us for receiving money from society, like most of us have to acquire educations, or to pursue our passions. On the whole, I'd like to think that we all give back as much or more than we receive. Don't single John out about his film grants. He happened to win several awards."

"I know, Petr, I went to the galas with you."

"So, what I'm asking, Patricia, is what does it matter?"

"I just wanted you to admit that you're okay with the status quo and you weren't going to advocate a mass culling of the poor tomorrow, Petr. I just wanted to know."

"I don't want to kill anyone. All the poor or just that one man and his children, either."

"Good, good, Petr. I just wanted to know. Pour me another glass of wine."

Excerpt from
"May 2nd Blog Part 1: S-Bahn, U-Bahn, We All Bahn"
(Blog post, May 2, 2011)

Basically, to explain the transit system here to a stranger, there are multiple ways to travel, all part of the same public system, so you can use the same ticket on different ways to go. The S-Bahn is the big commuter train that can get you long distances in a short amount of time. It actually shares its rails with the intercity and cargo trains, in a smart German sense of planning. They use intervals between S-Bahn trains to send the intercity trains through (or vice versa). Then there are the U-Bahn trains, which often run underground (though not exclusively) and are more designed for shorter, more urban trips. The S-Bahn and U-Bahn each have numerous lines with different routes. At major stations, both S-Bahn and U-Bahn lines come, though they use different platforms and you have to do a bit of figuring out which ones to go to. Luckily for me, there are lots of signs everywhere. Two key words to know are "Ausgang" (exit) and "Eingang" (entrance), as they are found throughout pretty much every large building, not just the stations.

To give you a taste of the routes I've been on, there has been the S41 and S42 (both are called the Ring lines, as they go in a ring around the centre of Berlin, with one travelling clockwise and the other counter), the U2 (an underground line that runs through the heart of the city), and the U6 (quickest route from my flat to Friedrichstrasse, basically the central hub of the entire network and walking distance to many of the attractions). Getting tickets is really easy, so long as you know what you are looking for on the self-service machines (as far as I can tell the machines are either only in German or I am too blind to find an English button).

The network is broken up into three zones, but for whatever reason zones A & B aren't separated in price fares. I've been told that unless I plan a daytrip to Potsdam (which I might) or a trip to the "other" airport, Schoenefeld (unlikely), I'll never need an ABC fare. So, with that in mind, my choices are really simple. A single trip AB fare costs 2.30 euros, while a day pass AB costs 6.30 euros. With the exception of the bus/train ride from the Tegel airport to my flat, when I used a single trip ticket, I've only been using day passes, though some days it is worthwhile and others I might have saved a couple euros by just doing the singles. Once a ticket is bought, you stick it in a validator and off you go.

Now, throughout the system it is largely an honour system, something I discovered five years ago the last time I came to Berlin and was mostly riding the S-Bahn four stops only. However, the last thing I want to do is be the guy who gets caught, and I have now actually witnessed others being caught. Forget the uniformed fare checkers on Translink in Vancouver; in Berlin they have plainclothes officers. A "dude" (either in reality or his costume) got on the U6 Monday evening, looking all nonchalant (or the German equivalent), waited until the train started rolling along and then flashed the badge. I pulled out my day pass. No problems, he moves on and finds a very clean-cut looking group of middle-aged adults and catches them without fares. At the next stop he tells them to get off. As far as I know he didn't give them a ticket, though I did see him give a different gentleman a ticket once he was on the platform. I'm not sure what the exact penalty is, but I've heard forty euros, which isn't awful, but I could afford to keep my money.

Beyond the S-Bahn and U-Bahn, there are also RE (regional) trains (similar to the S-Bahn, but more longdistance and require ABC fares), buses, and trams. I might take a RE if I go to Potsdam for a daytrip. I have no wish to ride on any more buses than I have to (it's the lowest form of public transport), but I might hop on a tram this week, just for the heck of it.

Trams are basically just as bad as buses, but have a mystique to them, and I don't mind experiencing a bit of that.

Excerpt from

"May 2nd Blog Part 2: Museum Boogaloo"

(Blog post, May 2, 2011)

"If you ever want to feel insignificant,
visit a museum."
– May 2, 2011
Berlin, Germany

I have always been a bit of a nerd. I know, it may come as a shock to all of you. But beneath the surface of this ultra-cool rock star writer, lurks a dude who likes to get his geek on. After spending most of the first few days in Berlin just trying to get a lay of the land, and waiting for a change of underpants, I hadn't yet got into diving into the rich cultural offerings the city had to offer. I knew that Labour Day Sunday meant that everything would be closed, so took the opportunity to enjoy the sun, sit by the Spree, and veg out. Sunday night, I decided I was going to get a jump on Monday, the new week, and start some sightseeing.

Unfortunately, due to the weather, so did everyone else in the city. Berlin is a city of about 3.8 million people, and about a billion tourists. I had already decided Sunday night I wanted to head to Museuminsel (Museum Island), as it was the home to a collection of world-class national museums.

I stood in line thirty minutes to get into the Pergamonmuseum. Who did I happen to see in the lobby? The Pan-European Elderly Tourist Locusts from the Frankfurt airport, that's who! I am not making that up. These weren't just people who looked and acted like those people, these were the very same people, right down to their red sweaters. Like I said, everyone was there.

Now the Pergamonmuseum is named after its star exhibit, the Pergamon Altar, a giant Greek shrine, which is the first thing one sees after entering the museum proper.

It is very impressive. I just can't say enough how impressive it is. It is a fantastic example of not only Greek architecture, but also carved art. Opposing the altar is a series of reliefs (in "frieze") that run around the main hall of the museum, depicting a great battle of the gods. As soon as you walk in and look up you are immediately thrown back.

Beyond the Pergamon artefacts, the museum also contains, Roman, Babylonian, Assyrian, and other relics of the "Ancient Near East". There is also a section devoted to Islamic art, including some beautiful calligraphic sheets depicting Iranian history and mythology. But, it is the big stuff that impresses me the most, and the Pergamonmuseum includes some pretty big stuff!

There is the Market Gate of Miletus, a Roman era merchant town that served as a link between Europe and Asia. It is also very big.

The only disappointing thing was to learn that the gate was the only thing grand, as the rest of the walls of the market were quite average. It was meant to be a large impressive facade to demonstrate the wealth and status of the city. I'm sure even visiting merchants could figure it out once they walked through and leaned up against a waist-high, see-through fence on the other side (note: may not actually be historically accurate).

No, for me, the thing about large gates, is that they need to back it up with some large walls. Luckily, also at the Pergamonmuseum was Babylon's Ishtar Gate. Nobody builds a good gate like the Babylonians, I always say.

Ishtar Gate is where it is at. Not only is it huge, it's pretty, too. I liked that it was blue and gold. I also liked the fierce animals just hanging around. Here's where your mind is about to be blasted. The reconstruction of the Ishtar Gate is actually just the LOWER portion of the gate. In reality, it was as much as two times as tall. And there were a whole lot of walls.

Nebuchadnezzar II (heard of him?) liked big things. He had a Processional Way, which was basically a big long road with really tall walls leading up to the Ishtar Gate. They reproduce the Way in the museum and it is really something else. And then they tell you that in actuality it was much, much bigger. Oh, and King Neb liked to have a message for his visitors. I can't remember this exact wording, but it was something along the lines of "Don't F With Babylon!"

Excerpt from
"Delicate Arms"
(Unpublished novel)

The afternoon takes forever to pass. It might have been the weather outside that made it seem so long. It seems like when the weather is awful I can just sit at my desk all day, without a care in the world. I would rather be indoors, anywhere, I suppose than face the gloom of the rain or the fog. Ottawa fog, that is. I don't mind occasionally ordering a London Fog at cafés. It is far more enjoyable than the weather, and the taste of Earl Grey and milk is most pleasant. I wonder if they have London Fogs in London?

Or, is it like we call Chinese food, a misnomer of geographic identification (and no, I don't mean with the overwrought use of the joke that they just call it "food")? I've been told that there are far too many regions of China, each with their own distinct traditions and flavours, that to go anywhere in Canada and order Chinese food is to be given Canadian ideas of what Chinese food might be. It is why there are such delicious delicacies as ginger beef, which does not exist in China (or did not originally), but gained great popularity in the Western provinces, due to their abundance of grade triple-A bovines. As I understand it, Chinese food, if one is searching for authenticity, is to be found at restaurants that advertise themselves under whatever regional specialisation they offer, with Szechuan being a regularly seen style, typified by its spiciness.

I could almost imagine a London Fog being created in some provincial outpost like Ipswich or Norwich, with the upwardly mobile merchant class trying to demonstrate their sophistication to the landed gentry.

"What have you got there, Cooke?"

"Oh, Lord Softbottom, I am just imbibing upon the latest of crazes to take the fashionable people of Westminster."

"What is it?"

"It's a frothy tea-based drink called a London Fog."

"It certainly looks like fog."

"Yes, Lord Softbottom, it does appear that way. But, let me assure you, it does not taste of fog."

"Of what does it taste, Mr. Cooke?"

"It tastes of Earl Grey."

"I know him! Let me have a sip, so that I might confirm its accuracy."

"Oh no, Lord Softbottom. I must have misspoke. It does not taste of Earl Grey, sir, but of the tea of his namesake."

"And what of Lady Grey?"

"I'm afraid I don't know what she tastes like, sir."

Eventually, I suppose I could see the second-born sons, without land to inherit coming to the colonies and spreading knowledge of their favourite beverage as they sit in public houses and coffee shops, waiting for the monthly receipt of allowance sent via Western Union.

"It's really quite a treat, back in jolly ol' England."

"I'll tell you once more, we have two options here. You can have some moonshine or you can drink the water. I'd recommend the moonshine. The last fellow who drank the water died of some horrible disease."

"So, no London Fog, then?"

In London, itself, though, it would only probably come to popularity with the industrial revolution, maybe, what with all the people flooding to the cities. There were bound to be a few incomers who arrived at the Thames with nothing but a few shillings and a desire to drink the soapy tea of their new home.

"Give me a London Fog!"

"A what?"

"Please sir, I have travelled day and night with promises of a good wage at a factory. I have uprooted my entire kin, and brought them to this strange and overwhelming city. Please, I beg you, just prepare for me that famous drink they call a London Fog."

"Listen 'ere, mate, I dunno what you's goin' on about, but we don't make nuffink of dat name 'ere, alright?"

"I believe it tastes of Earl Grey."

"I beg yer pardon!"

"The tea, sir, the tea. It is named after Earl Grey. They use the tea of Earl Grey and then do something with cow's milk, I don't know the whole process, but it comes out frothy and tastes of Earl Grey. Can you please make me one of those? They call them a London Fog."

"Are you havin' a laugh, mate?"

I was in a coffee shop once and ordered a London Fog and the girl smiled at me and asked if I had ever tried a Bombay Fog. I shook my head no, and then asked her what it was. She said that instead of Earl Grey, they use Chai tea. I have absolutely no doubt in my mind that the Bombay Fog does not exist in India.

"Vignettes (in Blue)"
(May 3, 2011)

- 1 -

"I've been standing here forever, what took you so long?"

"I'm sorry, there was an awfully long line at the women's washroom."

The man stared at the woman he had married two weeks ago and knew it had been a mistake. What had made him think it would be any other way? He had no idea.

"It's alright, I'm sure we have a long way to go before we're anywhere near the front of this line."

"Wasn't that group up there here when we arrived?"

He looked up ahead at the large group of elders and saw his own future.

A wild Thursday night had led to this, a tired Friday afternoon camped next to the toilet. Some unidentifiable insect scuttled behind the tank. He had felt so free, and now really felt trapped. He felt useless. He wasn't sure what kind of insect that was and whether it belonged by the toilet with him. Was it harmless? Or did it need to be eradicated? He wasn't sure. He just hoped that if he were to black out again, the insect would leave him be. At this point in life he was just relying on the kindness of his superiors.

- 3 -

Sat on the side of the dance floor, she watched her best friend twirl around with his girlfriend. Oh, those two danced. They smiled and cuddled. Kissed and tickled. All to the beat of the Baroque pop blasting through the retro speakers. He looked smashing in his trousers, white shirt and suspenders. His girlfriend was cute, but not outstanding. She wanted to have him grab her by the waist and spin her around. They could run away and start a pirate radio station. They could do all that if he only knew. And if he wasn't dancing with his girlfriend.

- 4 -

The sign on the bridge said no diving. The water was quite shallow. The current was quite strong. There were several more signs closer to the river's bank, on the grass. The weather had been fantastic that day.
The entire town was talking about it. An Indian summer, they call them. Like an extra bit of warmth that carries itself into the fall. It had been common to ride inner tubes in the river. People carried them down the side of the grassy hill and climbed in. The sign on the bridge said no diving. He will be missed always.

- 5 -

"You don't have to if you don't want to. I'm not going to force you. I would never do that. It's all completely up to you. Okay? Is that clear?"

"Yes."

"Good. How does that feel?"

"Nice."

"Let me know if I'm hurting you, okay?"

"Okay."

Those words scrolled through her head every night since. He didn't hurt her, not physically anyways, and not on that night. He just walked away afterwards and pretended not to know her. She saw him a few weeks later. She tried hard to make eye contact with him, but he just walked right by.

- 6 -

She could take no more. The child would not stop its behaviour. Every book she had read, all of their instructions on how to handle these situations, had proved useless. This terror would not stop. So she let it go on. She could take no more of it on her own, so she did nothing to stop it from exploding into the outside world. They all looked at her, wondering what an awful parent she must be. It wasn't true, she wanted to shout back, but she knew she couldn't lie. She sat back and watched failure progress one generation.

- 7 -

"Do you love me?"

A heart wants to know that it is not alone in the world.
It cries out for reassurance, hoping that the one it is with
now, will be the one it will be with forever.

"No. I don't think that I do."

A mind decides that it does not want to be with the one it
is with now forever so it makes a statement of inevitable
termination.

"Sure, of course I do."

A penis decides that it has enjoyed their companionship
and would like to continue it for the time being.

Hearts will be broken.

- 8 -

Every night they'd go to their special place. Between them was a tall stonewall that divided their properties. He was young and ambitious and knew that he must go further away from here. He promised to take her. She was the youngest of a protective warlord, a man who was not to be crossed. He didn't let her out of their compound. The young man knew from their conversations that he needed to take her away with him. On the night of his departure, he bribed the gateman to let her out. He was disappointed when he saw her finally.

- 9 -

"Roses for sale!"

The beggar woman called out on the city streets.
It was Saturday and the whole world was about.
She had collected fifty of the most wonderful red roses
and wrapped them carefully in cellophane.
Standing outside a bar she found a few young couples
with generous hearts and fivers to spare.
The girls giggled as their boyfriends handed them their
gifts. The poor beggar woman couldn't help but
remember being their age. So much to look forward to.
So much life to live. It seemed like it was just yesterday a
young man bought her a rose.

- 10 -

He left the classroom and headed down the underground
hallway towards the main open grass area, the quad,
it was a sunny day when he had gone underground for
his class and he was looking forward to seeing it again.
Opening up the door he walked past a group of smokers.
Normally not bothered, he had noticed they were very
close to the doorway and the law required a distance of
nine metres. Turning to tell them off, he realised that he
saw his own girlfriend having a drag.

"I didn't know you smoked."

"No? Oh, well I do, sometimes."

- 11 -

"I love you."

A heart makes a declaration, throwing itself out into the air, aiming for its target and hoping to be received in return.

"Oh."

A heart has been crushed by the realisation that it had been in a one-sided relationship.

"I guess I love you too."

A heart hears its opposite shrug.

"That's fantastic."

A heart can see the rubber ball bounce away.

"Je t'aime, aussi."

Un cœur est content, mais seulement pour quelque mois. Apres la, le cœur a pensé pourquoi est-ce qu'il parle de français?

"I love you too"

A heart heard it before can't believe.

- 12 -

A man sits on a park bench. He's dressed in his finest.
The sun pours down on him and he wipes his forehead
with a handkerchief. Joggers run by in their short
fluorescent shorts. Birds chirp and peck at fallen
breadcrumbs. The man checks his watch nervously.
His fingers tap, involuntarily, on the top of his knee.
He stands up and looks in both directions. He checks the
information post nearby to assure himself he's in the
right place. He is, and has been for quite some time.
He goes home to find a blinking light on his answering
machine.

"I'm sorry, but it is better this way."

He reads the letter over and over again, trying to decipher some special meaning from it all.
An empty dresser and chest of drawers. The spot where the dog's kennel used to rest. There is a box by the front door that says someone will pick it up on Wednesday. Who is someone, he wants to know. How could it be better this way? On what planet is this going to be better? It was at that moment, in reading her letter again, he realised that she had meant it for herself.

- 14 -

They flirted for months while he was away. It was like the old days. It might have even felt better than the old days. All the hurt and pain was gone. He was returning and she was excited to see him. She had told him she was driving down for the weekend. He didn't know what to do. It all seemed so real. It was finally happening.
And there she was, a ray of beauty. She smiled and gave him a hug. He smiled back and asked how she was doing. She turned to one side and introduced her boyfriend.

- 15 -

There was nothing left to say between them. It was over months ago, they just needed to exchange a few things. He had some of her stuff and she had some of his.
A neutral meeting place was chosen, halfway between their homes, to make it fair for driving. She seemed unaware of the irony of the location. He tried not to remember their first date as he handed over her things. It was over in less than five minutes. He walked out of the Cineplex and onto the front step where she had hugged him that very first time.

- 16 -

The sun rose and the sun set. It repeated itself like this everyday, of course. For most people this marked a differentiation in their lives. Some people worked during the day and slept during the night. Others, with different schedules had to do the reverse. He, as a decidedly different case, did not work, nor did he sleep. He just sat on his sofa, weeping. His mother would bring him a cup of tea. His father would invite him outside to go for a walk. He wouldn't move an inch from that sofa.
He was just the boy who wept.

- 17 -

She wore a frock and danced a scattered, haphazard dance. She was free and alive. He just watched her from a distance, too petrified to make a move. There was a group of people there. He wasn't sure if that made it easier or harder for him to talk to her. He counted the bodies and the girls outnumbered the guys. She danced alone. Why could his feet not move? He got off of the barstool and started walking. Her eyes met his and she smiled. He smiled timidly back as he passed her, the group, and left the club.

- 18 -

The gallery was filled with modern and post-modern pieces that interested the two of them. Neither was pretentious, though they each had their own peculiarities, as is the norm these days. He was enthralled with the photography. She was enthralled with the paintings. They followed the viewing with a fantastic lunch, where they laughed and discussed both the meaningful and the trivial. After that they walked down the street, pointing at things of note. When it came to be that time, they hugged in a friendly, innocent manner and went home to their significant others. They both wondered what if?

- 19 -

He'd never killed a man before. He wasn't sure if anyone would say that he did this time either. He felt awful either way. There were certain feelings that one can't ignore in the body. He had been so sick that he had to be escorted to a washroom to purge his lunch.
Unlike a normal act of vomiting, this one came with no relief. How could this have happened? He did not wake up that morning with the intention of causing a man's death. He was convinced that the man was innocent and that his jury had been wrong.

- 20 -

"Will you call me?"

"I promise I'll call you every night."

"You promise?"

"Yes! Of course, I do!"

"Because I just want to hear your voice before I fall asleep."

"There's nothing I'd want more either, honey."

"I love you so much."

"I love you too, baby. It's only a short trip."

"And you'll call me every night?"

"Yes, yes, of course!"

"I love you!"

"I love you! Talk to you later."

Every moment that they had spent together ran through his mind as the plane went down. He felt awful that it wouldn't be him calling her that night.

"They say that you're a morose bastard."

"That's probably true. I don't know what people say about me."

"Would you say it's true?"

"I thought I just did."

"No, I think you just acknowledged that people say things about you."

"You've got a real smart mouth on you."

"I try."

"Are you sure that you want to do this?"

"You're not as much of a bandit as I expected."

"I just have my qualms, that's all."

"Is one of them defiling the sheriff's daughter?"

"It depends on why you're so keen."

"Let's just say I have my reasons."

"Fair enough."

- 22 -

Every day, there is an old man who sits at the foot of a tree. He comes and leans against it and slides himself down. He spends all afternoon just sitting against the tree, looking out at the world, almost defiantly.
One day, he wasn't there. That turned into two, and then three days. A week passed before the old man returned to sit against the tree. When he returned, he did like he always did and put his back to the tree trunk and slid himself down. He cried that day looking at the orange paint encircling the tree.

- 23 -

They stood in the incomplete home and laughed at their mischief. The house had been framed and plywood had been put up. One of the boys laughed as he found a caulking gun lying on the unfinished floor. Taking it to the edge of a door, he stamped his foot down, watching the caulk explode. The other boys just watched and laughed. It wasn't until the boy was walking home, away from his friends, that he showed his shame. Parked in the driveway was a beat-up pickup truck and the boy knew that he would get what he had deserved.

He sat on the patio and ate an overcooked hamburger.
It had been a great afternoon by the pool. The group of
friends had swam and laughed. The barbeque had finally
worked and then with the hamburgers, overworked.
He couldn't put his finger on what was wrong until he
looked at his friend, who was looking with lusty eyes at
their host, while his friend's partner sat to the side
oblivious. It was at that moment that he knew that his
friend was in love with their host. He ate the overcooked
hamburger and wondered if his friend knew too.

- 25 -

There was a still a stretch of the original wall left, kept for preservation and remembrance. Rather than to glorify the previous regime, artists had been given space to paint murals, which almost universally sent positive messages. On one mural was a picture of two hands reaching over the wall, touching each other, almost as if they were to pull each other over this insurmountable obstacle. That's what it looked like, perhaps, before a vandal had splashed a bucket of blue paint across the wall and rode off on their bicycle (their tires left a long trail of blue paint).

"The Arch"
(May 4, 2011)

Save a moment for a weary old face, won't you? Yeah,
that's it. Just sit there and let me sit next to you. I just
want to say so many things. I suppose they've all been
seen before. I can see it in your eyes that you want
nothing more but to walk away. Fight that impulse!
Please, I ask you, just stay for a moment with a man
who has nothing left to his name. It's a terrible place to
sit, I know, but I think you have it in you. I know that.
I really do believe it. There's a few good apples in every
bunch, you just have to sort through them to find them.
You know that, don't you? Yes, you know. I can tell that
you do that exact thing at the supermarket. You go to the
rack where they display the galas or the golden
delicious's, I know you do. You walk up to the rack and
you start pick and choosing to find the few good ones.
I know you do. It's like that with finding listeners for a
tale. I can say that most people just want to ignore a
man with a story, but I can see that you're a good apple,
so to speak. So, please, a moment, or two, for a weary
old face. It will be worth your time, I can hope to promise
you that. I really can. I'm glad you've stayed. Let me get
on with the story.

Back in the days of my youth I used to hang around a
café. It wasn't much to mention, a fairly unremarkable
locale. There were tables on the outside patio with
striped umbrellas and on the inside there were small
round tables with wrought-iron chairs. That sort of place.
You can imagine it now, no? Good. Back in those days,
I wasn't much to look at, but I tried to carry myself with
confidence and swagger. A man has to work with what
he's given, see, and I had consigned myself to the fact
that I wasn't going to turn any heads on my looks alone,
so I'd have to get by on charm. Now, you may be
suspecting that this is a tale about me charming some
young girl. I can understand your trepidation, but it's

nothing of the sort. At least not below the surface. You see this story starts with a girl, but that's the way stories go, at least in my mind.

Her name was Evelyn. It was the summer of my seventeenth year and everything seemed possible. I had just made captain of the first XV and was itching for fall to come. There were a few training sessions with the lads, but nothing too strenuous. The workload was low and everyone was afraid of the heat. More time was spent sitting on the patio of the café, sipping on sodas and talking about birds. It was in one of those bull sessions, I was with Sammy Barlow, Reggie Scott, and a fellow everyone called Brick, though no one remembered his Christian name (I had suspected it was Brennan, but wasn't sure), that we saw her.

Evelyn Andrews was fifteen; with a birthday around Christmas, and a habit for smoking menthol cigarettes that made everyone forget her age. I had seen her around town before. I don't think she went to our school, but the private academy around the corner. I remembered that earlier that year she had been seeing Mike Dowd, a fellow in the year below who had come out to a few practices before quitting for football. It didn't matter, as it goes, as he was never able to break it into the starting eleven, as the school manager never could find a use for him. He wasn't tall enough to be a target man, skilled enough to play a midfield role, and his positioning was so poor it was out of the question to play him at centre back. Come to think of it, we didn't have much use for him either. It was these sorts of things that made it all the more perplexing when Dowd arrived at the Spring Formal with Evelyn on his arm.

I remembered that when we were sitting on the café patio that summer and she rode by on her bicycle. I don't know who it was first, maybe Brick, or possibly Reggie, but someone shouted out at her. I can't remember what was said but she rode by with a frown on her face. It was too bad as she was looking really good. I think she was wearing a summer dress with a cardigan sweater over the top. She had definitely piqued my curiosity, which isn't too much, really, in retrospect to mention. A seventeen year old will notice just about any female form in the heat of summer. But Evelyn was a cut above the rest. I just knew it.

Disappointed that she had rode by, we carried on with our bull session. Barlow had made a bet that Brick wouldn't jump off of St. Michael's bridge. The bridge was a tall, single arch that crossed the river that dissected the town. It was considered a bit of a rite of passage just to walk across the arch, but more thrill-seeking (or foolish) folks chose to jump. Brick was balking at the idea, and it took some prodding from Reggie and me to get him to seriously consider it. He was begging for a wager to make it worthwhile, his manhood apparently not large enough of a reward for him. Barlow egged him on by bragging that he, himself, had actually walked across the arch. He said that he had actually done it the previous winter, after New Year's and had done it wearing dress loafers without much grip, to top it all off. The way he saw it, Barlow was now the alpha male in the group until someone could top his feat. Brick had always considered himself the unofficial leader of the group and that was rubbing him the wrong way. He didn't like that no one had actually seen Sammy walk across the arch. Worse, though, he didn't like the thought that Sammy Barlow was now the leader of the group due to his (un-witnessed) act of manhood. Obviously, there was no way for Brick to walk across the arch and one-up Barlow. If he did it now, he'd always hear about how Barlow had done it across the icy steel in winter, without so much as a proper sole. That burned him up. Barlow knew that it did and that's why he had made the wager that Brick had to jump. He knew that it would be the only thing that Brick could do to top his own act. He also knew that Brick knew it too.

While Barlow continued to egg Brick on, I took the opportunity to head inside the café to relieve myself and to grab a milkshake. I was on my way along the far wall, towards the washrooms, when just passed the jukebox

I ran into Evelyn Andrews. I just smiled and tried to keep walking. She stepped in my path and looked me in the eyes. She spoke and said that she knew who I was. I didn't know what to say to that, so I just mumbled something meaningless. She asked if I had been sitting on the patio with the guys who had shouted at her on her bicycle. I meekly said yes, that had been my friends. She frowned, quickly, and then turned her face into a smile again, as if it really didn't mean anything. We started talking a bit. Apparently shortly after the guys had shouted at her, she had parked her bike around the side of the café and entered through a back door that the baristas used for smoke breaks. I learned that Evelyn liked to go for a ride roughly the same time everyday during the summer as it coincided with when her mother watched her favourite soap opera. Evidently the woman liked to scream and howl at the television in reaction to the story arcs and drama. She had even written a few sternly worded letters to the broadcasters. During the school year Evelyn didn't have to put up with it, but the summer, with the humidity, was unbearable. So she rode her bicycle down the various lanes and side streets of our neighbourhood, with no particular aim or really much speed at all, either. It was just an excuse to get out of the house for an hour.

I noticed that I had been standing there for what seemed like ages and mentioned that I was on the way to the loo. She smiled, unembarrassed, and asked if I'd like to meet up with her later. I shrugged and said okay, as I had nothing to do. I thought about it a second and followed my acceptance with a question. I just wanted to know if she was still seeing Mike Dowd. She smiled, again unembarrassed, and said no. I said I'd meet her outside the park's north gate at seven. She said that would be swell and turned around and walked over to the café counter.

At quarter to seven, I was tying up the laces to my sneakers when my kid brother came out of the front room and inquired what I was up to. I said it was none of his business. Right? I know you'd do the same if your nosy younger sibling wanted to know every single detail of your life. It had been unbearable the past school year as we were in the same school for the first time in years. I told him to get lost and left home. From my parents' house to the north end of the park is almost a straight walk, with only a couple turns. The last stretch of it is downhill and I could see from about two blocks away that Evelyn was already waiting for me by the gate. Once she noticed me, I waved at her. She waved back and smiled.

I don't remember what I did next. I think I may have hugged her and possibly kissed her on the cheek. I don't remember it well at all. I do remember that she was looking as stunning as I had seen her earlier that day, perhaps even more so. It was hard to imagine it, but when she rode her bike, in that flowing summer dress, it seemed as if sunshine emitted straight from her. It created an angelic vision, completed with her brown hair flowing in the wind. That afternoon, on foot, she looked every bit as miraculous. She didn't need a bicycle or the wind for props. She was angelic.

We walked through the park, as it was still daylight, and talked about all manner of nothing, the way teenagers do. She asked me if I had heard of a musical group that she liked. I remember answering that I hadn't but I would definitely try and check them out. I can tell you now that I did, not too long after that night and she was right. They were really quite something. I wish I could remember the name of them. I think they made it big a few years later. It was amazing that Evelyn had seen it coming. She must have had her finger on the pulse, because we talked about music for maybe an hour and I don't think I contributed anything to the conversation other than the occasional agreement or a prodding for more information. I briefly talked about rugby, but I could tell that her eyes glazed over and that she wasn't interested in sport. I quickly moved on to the latest gossip that had been sweeping through town. She had heard the rumours about Ron Baker and Louise Shipman. I didn't know whether it was all true.

I had known Ron from some of my classes and he just didn't seem like the type of guy to let something like that happen. Evelyn just repeated what she had heard. She didn't really know Ron or Louise. She had a friend who had been dating Louise's younger brother, but that was last fall and it had been too long to really be able to say anything definitive.

We walked through the entire length of the park and reached the river's bank. Sitting on the grass, we talked about the upcoming school year. I said I was excited to be finishing, but nervous about what came next. Evelyn just laughed and said she was jealous that she didn't have that problem. As she put it, she still had two more years of scholastic hell, before she probably embarked on a journey into a deeper layer of hell, whether it was more school or marriage. It was strange for me to hear those words come out of her mouth, because it sounded as if she had already seen her future. I hadn't really thought much beyond the next year. I was too preoccupied with the upcoming season and my duties as captain to even consider that life would exist beyond school. At that moment I knew I had to start living, so I turned to Evelyn and kissed her on the lips. After a short pause she reciprocated and we spent the next fifteen minutes making out on the grass.

We would have continued, I want to believe, had it not been for the commotion of sound we heard on the other side of the river. I sat up and looked across, only to see the familiar faces of my friends, Sammy, Reggie and Brick kicking pebbles and walking towards St. Michael's bridge. Evelyn sat up and noticed them too. She asked me what was going on. I told her about the wager that Sammy had made with Brick. I said that they were probably heading to the bridge so that Brick could make a point and jump. She laughed and said that we were all so stupid for needing to prove our manliness to each other. I wanted to agree, but there was a part of me that was beginning to believe that my rank in the group was slipping, and at this rate, fast. It didn't seem to matter much to them that I was the captain of the first XV squad. Reggie had quit rugby last fall, mostly due to his shoulder, but also because his mother didn't care for the violence. Sammy and Brick just didn't seem to treat me with the respect the post might have demanded, but I suspect that was more to them being friends with me forever. No, if our pecking order was to be decided, it was to be decided by activities within the group. In that respect, Brick jumping off St. Michael's bridge would be a declaration to the rest of us.

Not wanting to miss this spectacle I goaded Evelyn into walking to the bridge and meeting the boys there. She pecked me on the cheek and we walked hand-in-hand towards the bridge. When we arrived, Barlow was throwing every known insult at Brick's manhood. The guys cheered when they saw me. Recognising Evelyn from earlier they each extended their welcome and apologised for their behaviour at the café. Evelyn smiled and told them not to worry about it. She asked them what was going on. Barlow explained that he had walked across the icy arch last New Year's wearing dress loafers and that the only way for Brick to beat that would be to jump off the bridge. Brick at that point looked very nervous, perhaps aware that there was an outside witness. Barlow kept hurling insults at Brick, occasionally throwing out an empty apology to Evelyn, whom he didn't try to meet eye to eye. Reggie sat on the side rail and with only the slightest of efforts tried to encourage Brick to jump. I don't remember what I was doing at the time, though I'm sure I could have been capable of joining in with the encouragement of Brick. It all seems like such a blur, now. I tell you, it's hard to believe.

In all that noise and hollering nobody seemed to notice Evelyn. She had scurried up the main arch of the bridge and was now directly above us. She waited until the yelling at Brick died down for a moment and then quietly spoke. She looked each of us in the eyes, one by one, and said that she thought that our contest was stupid. She looked at me and smiled. And then she jumped.

Excerpt from

"Delicate Arms"
(Unpublished novel)

I sit on the balcony of my apartment with a cold beer in hand. There is just something right about this one singular experience. I don't know why humans created alcohol, but in the right doses it certainly enriches our experiences. My senses buzz a little, and my head gets a bit cloudy and everything becomes a bit calmer. There is no need to fret or worry, not after a few drinks, and well before too many. No, it is all well and fine. There is, I might say, a stillness to it all. It's as if the world has stopped or at least slowed down long enough for us all to be alive and to taste it. To smell it. To feel it. To hear it. All the senses get a bit more alert, for a bit, and everything is as it was meant to be. I've heard some say that alcohol was created to be in unity with the gods. Bacchus, the god of wine, descends to earth and creates merriment and wonder. In our festivals, our carnivals, our symposiums, our dances, and in our balls, we just want to reach up to the heavens and be one with them.

It's a warm, late spring day and a small flow of air wipes against my brow. I look out from my balcony and see large white, noble clouds charging past. They're heading east from here. I raise my bottle and toast the sky. I bid the clouds farewell and hope that they spread their goodwill to my friends, my brothers and my sisters, to the east. I bid good wishes to them in Montreal. I want nothing more than hearty laughter in Quebec City. Onward, clouds, onward you must go. Spread good cheer to St. John's, though I doubt they need any encouragement.

Then I am left with an empty bottle. Then I am left alone. The clouds have passed me by. They have taken Dionysus on their shoulders and departed.

I look out from the balcony and see the vacant side street, with barely a soul around. I turn to peer through my sliding glass door and observe the quiet, empty apartment I call home. I've heard others, still, say that alcohol was created to escape thoughts of the gods.

"Wounded Youth"
(May 6, 2011)

Ellie watched the minute hand tick closer towards its peak. That would be its end before it resets itself and begins another downward spiral. She glanced down at the desk and the booklet in front of her. The exam was complete. It was a terrific feeling, if slightly anxious. The year had come and gone. So quick, she thought. This time last year she was sitting in her spare block, gossiping with Janine. They would dish about who was sexually active and who was a prudish cocktease. It seemed childish now.

Eight months of university had brought about a lifetime of experience. Janine had coyly hid her summer affairs from Ellie and entered the school year with a flirtish confidence. Ellie had staidly worked at the grocery store with the tenth graders. Her summer days were wasted away inside the air-conditioned store. Instead of the warm glow of the sun, Ellie's skin had failed to tan under the marigold paint of the chain supermarket walls. She wasn't sure, but there may have been the odd glance sent her way from male customers. Even then, Ellie thought it ridiculous that men would find her attractive. Her ill-fitting work shirt barely gave hints that she had physically blossomed. Who was she? She was naïve and inexperienced. Who could want that?

With no answers to the most difficult questions, Ellie took a guess. She scrawled together a string of random words, hoping they would cohere and form an argument. The exam was heavily weighted towards the essay section. It was a shame, Ellie thought, as at least with the opening multiple-choice section, she at least had a twenty-five percent chance of being correct. It lulled her into a false sense of optimism. What they ought to mention is that there is the seventy-five percent chance of being wrong. Who would go with those odds?

Ellie had the solace of knowing that there were no penalties for incorrect answers in the exam. She walked to the front of the room and turned over the booklet. Summer had arrived.

Harry waited for Ellie outside the gymnasium.
He was listening to music and looking uninterestedly at his emails. Ellie skipped ahead and caught him by surprise with a kiss on the cheek.

"Hey handsome."

Harry took one headphone out of his ear.

"Oh, hey Ellie, how'd the test go?"

"Not bad. I'm glad it's over, though. Where do you want to go to celebrate?"

"Oh, sorry, did I not tell you?"

"Tell me what?"

"A few of the guys are going out for pints."

"Okay, I guess we could go with them."

Harry took the other headphone out and placed the player in his pocket.

"No, sorry Elle, I meant that I was going to go out for pints with them."

"What about our plans?"

"I didn't think we had plans."

"I thought we were going to go out for dinner to celebrate the end of exams."

"Yeah, okay, do you want to do that Sunday?"

Ellie looked at Harry to see if he was joking. He was not. She tried to hide her disappointment.

"Oh, Sunday. Yeah, I guess we could do dinner on Sunday."

"Great. I'll call and make reservations at Manitoba Grill."

"Manitoba Grill?"

"Yeah, I hear they have the best ribs in town."

"Oh."

"Don't worry, Elle, I think they also have salads and martinis and that stuff."

A month earlier, Ellie had mentioned that she thought she had put on a bit of weight during the school year.

"Okay, well, I guess we'll do dinner Sunday at Manitoba's."

"Great, Ellie. Anyways, I gotta run. Dan's meeting me at res in twenty minutes. I gotta hop in the shower."

He gave her a quick peck and jogged down the path towards the student halls.

"Call me."

**

Inside her residence room, Ellie sat on her bed, absent-mindedly reading a Jane Austen novel. Her lack of attention made it harder for her to remember which one she had picked up from the stack belonging to her Women Writers of the 19th Century course.
Among the Brontës, Rosetti and Eliot, Ellie had her favourite, Austen. Janine had teased Ellie for her fondness for Jane Austen. She said most of it came from a fondness for looking at Colin Firth brooding in period clothing. That certainly played a part, Ellie would admit,

but Firth's seminal portrayal of D'Arcy couldn't take away from the character himself, one of the reasons generations of young women have been drawn to Sense and Sensibility.

Where was her D'Arcy? Harry was not even close to meeting that ideal. Ellie knew that, but she also knew that she had great feelings for him. Harry had been a rock for her throughout this first year of university. How could she complain? He had even gone to her parents' house for all the major holiday dinners.

Even though her parents only lived in Orleans, Ellie had tried to distance herself from them during the school year. It didn't seem to work. Of course, as her father was a professor at the university, it was bound to occur that they might run into each other on campus occasionally. Ellie had just wished that it wasn't when she was with Harry. She felt uncomfortable holding his hand in front of her father. It wasn't that she was ashamed of Harry. No, it couldn't be that. Harry was certainly presentable. It just seemed off, to Ellie. Harry never mentioned it, but Ellie suspected that he noticed it every time. When they went for dinners at her parental home, Ellie always sat across from Harry. It seemed the easiest way for her to have to avoid touching him, or worse, him touching her.

The reverse situation was never a problem. Harry's family lived in Fredericton, too far to drive and too expensive to fly for a short visit. Harry's father came through the city on business once and took the three of them out for dinner. He seemed kind enough, and despite the overabundance of familiar in-jokes shared with his son in the presence of a stranger, Ellie felt welcomed enough. She even sat with her hand in Harry's.

Oh, Harry. She wanted him to be holding her hand right now. Her room was a mess and she needed to pack everything by Monday, residence checkout day.

It felt odd to have to leave a room that had been her home for the past eight months. It felt odder that she was to return to the house that had been her home for eighteen years prior, but now felt so foreign. Janine had laughed at Ellie for saying something along those lines last week.

"You're such an idiot, Ellie."

She was. She knew that. It had only been eight months but everything of significance in Ellie's life had happened in that room. She could remember her first night with Harry. They had been drunk enough, but not too much. She didn't regret it. She had welcomed him back after what passes for a date these days. Expectedly, he obliged. They sat on her bed and made out a bit. On her computer a romantic comedy was ignored. Harry's hands went exploring. Ellie could feel him getting anxious. She tried to put up a small show of propriety, but it was no use. She had wanted him since the first day of class when his blue eyes had met hers and asked if he could borrow a pen and a sheet of paper. What some might have called a complete lack of preparation for university, Ellie called boyish charm. He was no boy on that first night, though. Ellie could tell that Harry had been active for a while. He showed knowledge of what he wanted to do with her and also concern for her wellbeing in the process. He was firmly gentle. At that moment, Ellie was enraptured with Harry. Afterwards, lying in the sweat-soaked sheets, Harry put his arms around Ellie and cuddled her. She loved it.

**

Manitoba's was a really lame restaurant from the outside looking in. It was that appeal that had gained it credibility with the indie crowd, who went there "ironically". Janine had gone there on a date with a guy in skinny jeans to "re-appropriate the malaise of suburban milieu". They drank "shakes" and ate "hamburgers". Later that night, they had "sex", which Janine "enjoyed", and then told Ellie about.

Sitting there on Sunday night with Harry, Ellie wasn't feeling any of the place's so-called charms. There was a giant bison head above their table and the middle-aged busboy was depressing. Harry flipped through the plastic pages of the menu, unsure of what he was going to eat. Ellie had decided to have a chicken ranch wrap with a salad.

"What are you going to get, Elle?"

"Chicken wrap."

Harry frowned.

"Oh, really, you don't want to try the ostrich burger?"

"No. That's okay, a wrap is fine."

"They have a buffalo wrap, made from real buffalo meat, and slathered in buffalo sauce. It gets three stars in the menu."

"Why would the restaurant give grades to their own meals, Harry?"

Harry turned the menu towards Ellie and pointed to the ratings.

"See. And your chicken wrap only gets one and a half stars. That doesn't sound too promising."

"I can't believe that."

"They've got no reason to lie to us, Ellie, these ratings are voluntary, and if I were you I'd start looking at some food with a higher rating."

The waiter came to describe the evening specials and to take their drink orders. Harry ordered the restaurant's house beer ("brewed by buffalos, probably."). Ellie got a cosmopolitan.

"I'm really glad we could do this dinner, Ellie."

"Yeah, me too, I was wanting to celebrate the end of the school year. I'm so looking forward to the summer."

"Yeah, the summer."

Harry's face turned serious. Ellie did not like where this was going.

"I was thinking, lately, about the summer."

"Okay."

"I'm not sure what my plans are."

"That's okay, I'm not sure what my plans are, either. I was talking to my old manager and I might go back to the grocery store. Not sure."

"I'm not sure whether I'm going to stay in the city for the summer."

"Oh, alright, I guess we can work around that. I could come out to Fredericton over the May long weekend, and maybe you come up here for the week between St-Jean's and Canada Day, and then I go back over the August long weekend, and then you're back here for Labour Day."

Harry sat silent. Ellie continued, nervously.

"It's not ideal, obviously, but we could make it work. It's only four months, and we'd see each other once a month, minimum, right?"

"Yeah, I don't know if that's going to work, Elle."

"Alright, maybe I come to Fredericton for the summer. I've heard lots of nice things. That could be fun!"

"I don't know if I'm even going back to Fred this summer."

"Oh, so you could get a job in Ottawa?"

"No, Ellie, I don't know. I haven't decided what I want to do. I might travel a bit. I don't know. It's not really important where I am or where I'll be. I just think that we need to sort some things out."

"Oh no."

Ellie feared what he was about to say.

"Are you breaking up with me, Harry?"

"Elle, I don't know what to say."

"Well, say what you think we need to sort out."

"I'm just thinking that these past eight months have been great, but four months, a summer, is half as long as I've known you, and I'm not sure who I am going to be at the end of the summer or what I'm going to want in September. It's only fair that I am straightforward and honest with you."

"I see."

"I'm sorry, Ellie."

"You're sorry?"

"Yeah, I am."

"Why are we at Manitoba's?"

"This had to happen somewhere."

**

Dinner was almost ready, and Ellie's father was setting the table while her mother was checking the roast in the oven.

"Remember to set another place for Janine, dear."

"Right, almost forgot."

Ellie's father slid one of the place settings around the table to make room for an additional guest.

"What time is she arriving?"

"Should be here any minute, dear."

"I just wish we had been given a bit more notice."

"Nonsense, she's been a friend of Ellie's for years, she's practically family, George."

George grumbled something under his breath and finished with the forks and knives. He left the kitchen and plopped down on the couch. Looking over his shoulder to see that his wife wasn't nearby, George turned on the television and quickly pressed the mute button before any sound emitted.

"Come on, Tottenham, how did you do today?"

George flipped the TV to a pay channel that covered European sports to see how his favourite premiership team fared.

"Blasted!"

"What's that, George?"

"Oh, nothing Kathleen, I just stubbed my toe on the coffee table."

He turned the television set off and started walking back to the kitchen, where his wife had popped her head out to check on him.

"You alright, George?"

"Yeah, I'll be fine."

"I told you we should replace that thing. It's nothing but trouble."

"No, no. No need, Kath. Besides it goes with the side tables, I wouldn't want to mismatch."

"That's alright, we can just get a new set."

George frowned at the thought of the added expense. He went to the fridge to find a beer before his wife stopped him.

"Can you wait for dinner? I was thinking of opening a bottle of wine. It might be nice."

"Oh, okay. I just wanted a beer now."

"Well, have your beer if you want, but I don't want to open a bottle of wine if I'm the only one drinking it."

"What about Ellie and Janine? They'll help you out."

"You know, that's right. I didn't even think of Ellie being able to drink. That's something I'll have to get used to."

Sorting through the fridge in search of his beer, George had to push aside two cases of vodka coolers.

"Yes, I suppose I'll have to get used to it too."

The doorbell rang.

"Ellie! That'll be Janine!"

Ellie came bouncing down the stairs and opened the door.

"Hi, Janine."

"You're not wearing that, are you?"

Ellie was dressed in jeans with a conservative blouse, while Janine was wearing a short-cut summer dress with a significant amount of cleavage.

"What's wrong with this?"

"I thought you said you wanted to go crazy tonight. You look like you're ready for Bible study."

"I thought I looked good."

"You do look good. Too good. Squeaky clean good."

"That's not good is it?"

"No, that's not. Good is bad. Bad is good. You want to have a good time tonight and hook up you need to look bad. Am I clear?"

"I guess I'll change after dinner. You hungry? Mom made a roast."

"Awesome. I love meat. And so are you tonight."

"Quiet, Janine! My parents are in the kitchen."

"Oh, sorry. I'll keep it quiet that their daughter is planning to get shitfaced and fuck whatever guy she finds at the bar tonight, shall I?"

"You're awful. Just be quiet."

"I feel sorry for you, Ellie."

"Because I just broke up with Harry?"

"No, because you are too scared to be sexually liberated."

"It's not that. I am plenty, um, liberated. I just choose to be that way in the privacy of a bedroom, preferably with a man that is committed to me."

"That's a lot to ask tonight, love. I think you might have to consider having a quickie in the washroom."

"Stop it! If you're going to be like that I'm not coming tonight."

"If you dress like that, you certainly won't be."

Ellie gave a stern look.

"Alright, I'll behave. At least while we're having dinner."

The girls join Ellie's parents in the kitchen. Kathleen gives Janine a hug.

"Oh my, Janine. You look dressed to impress tonight. Isn't she, George?"

George just mumbled something vaguely approving.

"Come on, George, give her a look."

The middle-aged professor looked at Janine in the way a middle-aged professor usually looks at attractive girls his students' age: disinterested lust.

"Yes, you look very nice, Janine. Though, I should say you're not really matched well with Ellie."

"Oh, that's okay, George. Ellie's getting changed after dinner."

George frowned a father's frown.

"Oh. Do sit down. I'll go see where your brother is, Ellie."

With her husband out of the room, Ellie's mother asked the important questions.

"Where are you going? When are you coming home? Will you take your phone? Do you need any cab fare?"

"A bar. Never. No. Please."

Kathleen smiled as she handed over forty dollars.

"It was worth asking, Elle."

"You know I've been living out of this house all year and never had to answer those questions."

"Yes, I know. Sorry, it's just hard for me to get used to my little girl growing up. I mean look at Janine, no offense, but I saw that girl grow up five years ago."

"It's true, Kath."

"I just always thought of you as my sweet little angel and to think of you going out to a disco, wearing high heels, dancing with men, it, well, it just seems so soon to me."

"I know, Mom. I do, I really do. But if you think we're going to a disco, you really do need to get with the times. Nobody calls them that any more."

"To be honest, Kath, I don't think they were still called that when you were our age."

"Thank you, Janine. Ellie, be safe. That's all I ask."

George returned to the kitchen, accompanied by his sixteen-year-old son.

"Kyle, you are looking good, big man."

"Thanks, Janine. You look like a slut."

"Gimme your allowance and I'll show you."

George cleared his throat. Ellie shoved her friend. They all sat around the table while Kathleen served the roast.

**

The bus downtown was packed with tons of people. Janine had found a spot for the two of them in the back. Ellie sat, wearing the outfit her friend had selected, feeling particularly self-conscious and a little bit cold from the draft. At Blair Station, she watched a small group of guys get on, hopping on at the middle of the articulated bus, squeezing themselves in. She recognised a couple of them as friends of Harry and wanted to disappear into her seat.

"What's wrong, Elle?"

"Quiet. It's nothing. I just know those guys."

"So? Some of them are kinda cute."

"They're friends with Harry."

"That would be delish, Elle. You should totally hook up with one of them."

Ellie was beginning to have major doubts about her plans for the evening. It had seemed like such a good idea when she and Janine had cooked it up the night before in a sea of gin and tears.

"I don't want to talk about that."

"No worries, just let it go, 'kay? There will be plenty of guys at the bar."

"Yeah, I know. I just don't want to think about Harry or this won't work."

"Right. You got it. I won't bring it up from now on. Let's only think about good things."

"Thanks, Janine. You're a good friend."

"I'm only half the friend you are, Elle."

Janine put her hand on Ellie's freezing arm. The two met eyes and smiled at each other. Ellie's concerns started to work themselves out. The butterflies stopped flapping at the same rate, anyways.

**

"So, what do you study?"

"I haven't really decided on my major yet. I don't know what to concentrate on. I've enjoyed the lit class I've taken. Maybe English?"

"That's cool. I always enjoyed English."

"How old are you, again?"

"I'm twenty-five."

Ellie looked at him and had her doubts.

**

The strobe lights were flashing an irregular beat while the bass thumped a steady, comforting one-two-three-four. Ellie lifted her feet up and down, back and forth, thrusting her pelvis in and out. She could feel his hands working their way up and down her sides. As she pushed her waist out she could feel his body grinding up behind her. She threw her arms above her head and twirled her hands in a rhythmic rotation. His hands groped her waistline and continued below, pulling Ellie tighter. The heat in the bar and the dancing had caused them both to work up a sweat. Ellie reached backwards with one of her arms, and let it slide down, across his face, down his chest and she started groping his leg. He dipped his body and his t-shirt stuck to the back of her top. Ellie's hand felt his firm, but sweaty abdomen.

She turned to face him; her one hand still nestled beneath his t-shirt, and grabbing his head with her free hand, pulled the stranger in and kissed him.

Ellie then pulled away and danced freely to the pounding drum and bass. The stranger put out a hand, took Ellie's and pulled her close to him. He leaned forward, slightly to the side and whispered in her ear. He couldn't see it, but she had an expressionless face as she nodded.

**

Working their way through the crowded bar floor, Ellie saw Janine in the distance. She wanted to call out to her, but before she knew it they were at the coat check.

After collecting their things, the stranger's jacket, Ellie's purse, the newly acquainted couple stepped out to the curb. In what seemed like no time whatsoever, the stranger had flagged down a taxi and Ellie was riding off to a certain end.

**

In the stranger's condo, Ellie could tell that whether he was or wasn't twenty-five, he had a fair bit of money. The floors were a dark stained hardwood and the counters a white marble. All of the appliances looked brand new and Ellie thought she could almost see her reflection in the stainless steel. She thought she saw a young girl, but as her clouded mind cleared with the glass of water the stranger offered, Ellie could see quite clearly that she was, in fact, a woman with only one aim. Her face wore a small pout. Isn't this what she wanted? No time to doubt, it, Ellie. No time for that.

The stranger asked if Ellie wanted anything else to drink or eat, if she wanted to sit in the living room, if there was anything at all he could do for her. He seemed genuinely sweet, this affluent stranger with the firm sweaty abdomen. No, Ellie refused all of those offerings. She asked him where his bedroom might be and if he would like to show her. Slightly taken aback, the stranger smiled and led Ellie down the long corridor, past the laundry and the washroom, past the linen closet, past the office, and past the guest bedroom to where the master suite lay.

Ellie pushed the stranger onto his bed. He smiled with surprised delight as he didn't expect this seemingly timid creature to be so direct or forceful. Ellie ran her hands down the strangers chest, grabbed the bottom of his designer t-shirt and pulled it up to his head. Had he not reacted and cooperated with his arms, Ellie was in such a mode that she might have left the stranger with his head covered. Next she moved to his belt and pulled the length of leather from the buckle, unzipped his blue jeans, grabbed his waist and pulled the pants right off. Without much ceremony, Ellie slipped out of her skirt and top, popped off her bra and took off her underwear. She climbed onto the now much expectant stranger.

**

The stranger was snoring on the other side of the bed. Ellie quietly slipped out, grabbed her clothes and shut the bedroom door. Putting on her clothes with the same quickness she had taken them off just a few hours ago, Ellie was out the front door of the condo in half a minute. She walked maybe two blocks and then stopped. She looked up at the night sky. It wasn't even all that dark any more. Perhaps her eyes had adjusted to the low light; perhaps it was soon to be dawn. It was hard to tell. She could feel her eyes begin to water, but stopped herself from outright tears. Wiping her eyes with the side of her hand, Ellie persevered and walked to the nearest major intersection she knew. It was absolutely dead out. She reached into her purse and found her phone.

The clock said that it was four o'clock. Ellie sighed and dialled the number for a cab.

"The Fool"
(May 6, 2011)

"Gather round, gather round, and let's all raise a toast for the fool!"

"Calm yourself, Derek!"

"No, no, no. Calm myself, Derek, I shan't do that. I can't, my sweet, for I've been made a fool!"

"I won't listen to you while you're like this. You're drunk!"

"A fine observation, my sweet, a fine observation. But, even in my drunkenness, I know when I've been made a fool."

"I don't know what you're talking about."

"Him! Him! Him! How can you explain anything to me about not being foolish when I know that he's come into our home, like a thief in the night, to come and help himself to my beer, to sit on my sofa, to eat my biscuits, and to fondle my dear wife's breasts?"

"I really do not know what you're talking about, Derek. You must calm yourself."

"No! Never, my sweet. Honesty and decency were the only things I had to hold me together, since the incident, but this will surely destroy me! Who is he? Who is this charlatan, this philanderer, this conquistador of bosoms?"

"There is no one, dear, no one who is here."

"Then the coward has left! Fool! I've been made a fool! He's come into my home and taken comfort in my comforts in my absence and upon my appearance he absconds into the night's sweet air. A reckless fool, I've been. With the trust that I've shown to the world, this is how I am repaid. I show generosity and I am repaid in greed tenfold. A fool!"

"Really, Derek, you must calm yourself. There has been nothing of the sort. There is no one who is here or has been here other than yourself and I."

"What lies he's made you speak, my love. What horrible, awful lies. How am I to trust the delicate lips that I married so long ago, now? How can I live in this debased cottage, knowing that he lurks in the night, freely helping himself to good men's ale and their fair wives? How can I? Surely I've been made a fool of the highest order!"

"Let me draw you a bath. The ones with salt you so enjoy."

"Don't try and bribe me with frothy, soapy, mineral salt-laded baths, my sweet. I shan't be comforted by relaxing ointments or lotions, either. A fool! I've been made a fool and I need to fix this at once, or a fool I shall be until death."

"What will calm you? For my sanity, please, tell me."

"Ah! You speak! Finally you speak!"

"I've been speaking this whole time, Derek."

"You've been covering the tracks of your seducer, my usurper, the man who would cuckold my claims to manhood!"

"There is no seducer!"

"So you say he took you unwillingly? Dear Lord! That vile! That vermin! To the hangman's noose, we'll have to take him! It's one thing to impress a lady with seductive arts and win her affections, as uncomforting as it might be to a husband, but to force his body upon yours, oh no! We cannot have this! I'll rally a posse! We'll storm the hills at once! We'll find this dastardly creature and give him the sentence he so rightly deserves!"

"I have nothing more to say."

"No, of course not, my pet, you've been through a lot. You should go and lie down now. You should rest your weary, defiled body, and sleep, if your mind is not racing at a thousand revolutions. Yes, yes, my pet, nothing more needs to be said. I will hunt down this mad man and I will put an end to his gallivanting. There shall be no more of this. I will not rest until he gets his just dessert. In the highest hills and the lowest vales I will hunt him down. A crucifixion would be too good for him, to die as our Lord did. No, it shall be a disgraced hanging if he's to be brought to justice. We'll drag his syphilitic body into the town square and tie him to the hangman's stage. The crowds will come from the entire county to see this man who has made a fool of me, and likely also a great number of townsfolk and gentlemen, alike. We'll stand there in anticipation for his last words. I shouldn't be too optimistic, but I would not feel justified if he didn't mend his actions. I would hope that before every witness in the square he'd look me in the eyes and confess his trespasses against me. I'd want him to admit that he drank from my growler the last bit of ale. I'd want him to confess that he nibbled on my biscuits while he sat in my own home on my very own sofa. I'd want him to admit, though it would bring me much shame, I'd want him to admit that he fondled my wife's plentiful bosom, against her will, as it goes. Only then can justice prevail. Only then."

"Derek, you are a fool!"

"I knew it! You did have more to say! Your words betray you, my pet! You couldn't help but enjoy that vagabond's interest in your lady parts, could you? It's been quite a compliment for a woman of your age and station, hasn't it?"

"Dear husband, I'll ask you to stop! You are acting the fool, but you need not."

"Why is that, my sweet? Are you to tell me that you will be running away with the seductive usurper? Are you to tell me that you will take your plentiful bosom and its shame away? Am I to be released from this whole encounter as a lovable doofus? Am I to be a buffoon no more? Will I only be left alone to sit on my sofa chair, eat my remaining biscuits and weep?"

"You will do those things if you must. I only want to bring some clarity to your cloudy vision."

"Speak to me, my pet, for you have always been the voice of reason in this marital arrangement. Even when I had great ambitions to embark on a journey that might gain me fame and raise my name to the highest rafters, it was a foolish endeavour that you so wisely curtailed. Even when I had put an initial payment down on what I was told were legumes of magical properties, properties that might bring our family great fortune, you brought to my attention the possibility of fraud. I have many times been guilty of overstepping my boundaries as a man, but it is you that have kept me grounded with wise words. Speak to me, my pet."

"Derek, my dear, now that you are in a listening mood-"

"Go, on, yes."

"Now that you are in a listening mood I shall reveal your own foolery."

"I fear it is so, but my ears await the truth. I'll not erupt again, if you tell me of the cuckold."

"Just shut your overused mouth, my dear husband. Open those oft-absent ears and listen to what I have to say."

"Aye, my sweet."

"This whole scenario began yesterday's eve. You had finished your dinner and had retired to your sofa. I dutifully came and rubbed your shoulders. It had been a long and hard day for you. I could tell from the tension in your neck that it had been a strenuous day of toiling labour. I offered to draw you a bath, the ones with the mineral salts that you so like, but you declined. I continued rubbing your shoulders and you drifted into a bit of a slumber. No matter, I thought, I'll tidy the kitchen and make for bed, if he is so tired and in so much need of sleep. Without much notice, I turn around and you've began wandering around the house, but, and this may come as some shock to you, you were still asleep as far as I could tell. Your eyes were closed shut and you were muttering nonsense words. Not nonsense like you've been talking now, or when you found those magic beans, no, these were actually words without any sense to them. Words I had not heard before, not from your mouth, or anyone else's, not even the vicar. It was as if you were possessed by some foreign spirit and it was guiding you on your way without any hindrance from your body. You came to the kitchen and began opening the cupboards and pantry. You continued mumbling words of nonsense. Repeating things that I did not understand. Eventually, you found a corner of the pantry where small foods, snacks and that sort, are kept. Your possessed body, though it seemed independent from the man I married, most interestingly chose the very biscuits that Derek, my husband, would have chosen had he been awake. I was shocked and amazed, though I did not know what to do. I had never encountered a live spirit and I did not know what harm I might do if I were to startle it, that is, I mean, you. In your possession, you seemed capable of doing anything, that is, anything except leaving our home. For whatever reason, you would not leave. After eating the biscuits, which you did standing up in front of the pantry, over here, you just started walking around in circles. I didn't know what had come over you, but I thought it best not to interfere. You never know what a possessive spirit might do when startled, right? So I just let you continue in your strange, waking dreamlike manner. I let you go and grab your final growler jug of ale, it was yours after all, awake or not, and I stood aside as your body, in such a strange state, just reached out and grabbed my, well, you know, it grabbed my upper portions. Having just groped me, in a delirious sleeping state, your possessed body took the growler and plopped itself down on the sofa and drank until it was empty. It seemed calm at that point and then, as weird as it might sound for me to say this, then your sleeping body went to sleep, for real, though. It must have felt the effects of all that ale, because you were out cold, both your possessed body, and the man I married. You slept right through the night and well into the morning, until just now, you woke in a drunken stupor and began your faultless accusations. That is the truth, Derek, I tell not one bit of a lie."

"Are you mad, my sweet? That is the most unbelievable yarn I have ever heard, and remember I am a man that was convinced by the prospect of magical beans. Are you to expect me to believe that my honour was besmirched by the very hand that I possess?"

"No, Derek, your honour hasn't been besmirched at all. No one knows of these accounts. Like I said, for whatever reason you contained yourself to our home. You did not commit any foul greater than eating your own biscuit, drinking your own ale or fondling your own wife."

"You take me as some fool, don't you?"

"For your accusations, yes. But now that you've heard the truth, we can move on."

"No, a fool I shall remain. I want the truth! Where is that seducer? I shall lynch him for drugging me with some potion that knocked me out for so many hours, and I shall get my revenge for him poisoning you with whatever serum has made you speak such lies to your husband!"

"The Great Retreat"
(Blog post, May 8, 2011)

The sun is setting on the city and the streets grow quiet. Everyone is disappearing into their homes, the studio flats, and the tenements. After a long day of work and a bit of socialising at the street café or the beer garden, it's time to retreat. Retreat into the inner courtyards for a conversation and a short drag on a cigarette. Retreat into the apartment with the big open windows, only to hide behind bed sheets used as blinds, in that prole manner. Retreat to the outer suburbs. Retreat to Pankow. Retreat to Spandau. Retreat, retreat, retreat.

The all-hours doner kebab shop is taking a break. It's not closed, but there's no one around for a kilometre in any direction. The shopkeeper sips an ice-cold orange Fanta on the front stoop. It's eerily quiet. The city with an endless pulse seems to have slowed to the faintest possible beat. Everyone has gone into retreat. The clock strikes nine and the bells in the far distance can be heard with the utmost clarity. There is no traffic sound pollution right now. A night swimmer could take a plunge into Plotzensee and they would hear of it in Potsdam. Only a few of the older set, pensioners playing dominoes are out, and they are fading into the night.

At midnight, though, the mood changes with the date. It resets and everyone's energy is reset. At the U-bahnhofs outside the centre, there are signs of life, trickling in, bounding down the concrete stairwells and onto the platforms. Amidst the retreaters, amidst the tired, amidst the old, and amidst the infirm, there is life. The youth are gathering, and they are starting in the farthest corners, growing stronger in numbers as they move down the line and descend upon Warschauer Strasse and across the Spree in Kreuzberg. It's time for them to wake up and play. Below the surface of a clean and modern, proudly Western capital lurks an Eastern monster. In small groups, in good cheer, if slightly restrained, the youth murmur and ride the underground lines into the city centre. Changing lines means waiting, in fevered anticipation at another station. Finally, the U1 comes. The excitement can barely be contained. Everyone is in their own skin, putting on whatever appearance they wish. Next to the stiletto queens are the camouflage cargos. There is tiger print and blue jeans. Manolo Blahnik and Asics. Doo-wop poofs and punker spikes. Everyone is welcome to this party called Berlin.

Hands are filled with pre-club cheer. There is the ubiquitous Berliner Pils and its cousins, Schultheiss and Berliner Kindl. Some hands carry the pre-mixed drinks called Radler or Diesel. A few people carry Beck's and Erdinger. Stepping out at Warschauer Str U-bahnhof, there is a sea of people heading south to cross the bridge to Kreuzberg and another sea of people carrying the tide forward into Friedrichshain. Along the way, the currywurst and pretzel stands hock cheap eats and cheap beer to the marchers. Beggars and grifters, zealots and buskers, they all want twenty cents. A small boombox plays electronic music and stray partiers join in the dancing. The horde just keep moving forward, forward into the night, or is it morning?

Long gone are the hardships of centralised economics. Instead, it's a false nostalgia that spurs them on at Revelar Strasse, mere blocks from the largest slabs remaining of the Wall. Down into an open alleyway, the crowd descends and splinters, with factions heading into the various side gardens and warehouses.
Pop a head inside one place and see pleasant Caucasian Rastafarians tending bar at the front. They look as if they have been waiting for this particular evening, with these particular people to arrive. It's the youth and they are going to create something special tonight. It's what everyone has been waiting for.

Some people even went to sleep after work just to wake at midnight and hop in the shower. This place only really hits its stride after three, a girl exclaims. Out come the drinks and more Berliner Pils on display. Someone orders an Erdinger and gets it served in a long pint glass reminiscent of a vuvuzela. Prost!

One room is just a dark black box filled with black lighting and house music. A couple makes out on the ground. The next room, where the house music originates, is filled with vivacious dancers, unaware of ego or self-concern. They thrust themselves fully into the familiar house favourites of the past decade. Out the back door is a garden where a joint is indiscreetly passed around a circle. A casualty of starting on the pilsner too early is passed out next to a tree, a penis drawn on his arm in red lipstick.

Up the back stairs, a secondary entrance leads into a completely different scene from downstairs. Gone is the dark, in with the light. It's bright, everyone is clearly visible and different scenes are going on in different corners. On the dance floor hard cores and skaters, hipsters and clubbers, all get their feet moving and sing along with FM radio hits from 1998. There are miniskirts and combat boots. Sometimes on the same person. There are couches and the couple that had been making out downstairs are now grinding and dry-humping each other on the side couch. Across the room is a corner where a table football tournament is in play. Out come more drinks, large glass mugs, Jever, Club-Mate, Strongbow, and still more Berliner Pils. Prost!

The upstairs dance floor rumbles as the bodies bounce up and down. Everyone is jumping. They jump to Kris Kross! They jump to House of Pain! They jump to Van Halen! No one cares a lick about whether those songs or those bands are "cool" or not. There is no irony, only fun. It's a great song, man. It's a great song, man.

You've just got to like it. The room fills with the sticky sweat of fifty dancing fools and the smoke of fifty lit Pall Malls.

Back downstairs, the drum and bass is leading to feet blisters and transcendental experiences. How much higher can this go? How much higher can this go? They ask and plead the dance hall gods and are answered in a thunderous display. Out come the strobe lights. Out come the disco balls, long lying dormant. We going to take this higher! We going to take this higher! The grammatically incorrect chants lift the room's spirits and the euphoria erupts. The beats get faster and faster, their cadence drawing the room closer to completion. And then it drops. Sweet release, the souls of a hundred revellers on Revelar Str.

It carries on until the day breaks, and it is light outside. The lone vendor outside the U-bahnhof is making a fortune selling hotdogs, though he throws in a small packet of jelly candies. The trains keep running all night on the weekend, but there are long intervals. At Warschauer, the end of the U1 line, tired bodies and souls just lean against the plastic partitions, half asleep, half intoxicated. Some chow down on the overcooked sausage. Others laugh and explore each other's bodies. It's five o'clock, anyone who cares is fast asleep. Finally, the train starts and the retreat begins.

Excerpt from

"Delicate Arms"
(Unpublished novel)

Lunch came far too quickly today. I don't mind that when it happens, normally, as it provides a nice confidence boost that my indentured time is halfway over for the day. However, today I had forgot to pack a meal in the morning to bring. I hate the lunchtime rush at all the restaurants and take-away places. There are far too many suits. There are far too many banal conversations I might have to hear. No, let me scratch that, there are, in fact, far too many banal conversations I will have to hear. I can't remove myself from society, as Julian told me on Saturday. I have to be a part of this. But, if this is what it is, I don't want it. Maybe Rain Buttercup was right? She convinced Julian, at least superficially. Although, to be fair, Julian just wanted sex. Sex can trump everything. That must be why monks take vows of chastity and then move as far away as possible from young women. They want to believe and it's far easier to believe when your mind isn't clouded with thoughts of breasts and so on. My mind is far too clouded, these days.

Perhaps I too, could be a monk, living in a remote monastery. They could call me Brother Phillips, or Brother Edward if they are less formal. I suppose they might even call me Brother Eddie, but that might be too informal. I shouldn't care too much what they might call me. I'd probably take a vow of silence. That would help me from having to remember everyone's names.
I imagine there would be a lot of monks in a monastery. It wouldn't be easy to remember everyone's name.
As far as I know from my admittedly small to absent knowledge of monastic orders, there isn't a lot of variety in terms of haircuts or wardrobe. No, that would make it impossible to remember names. I suppose I could get by

for a few days calling everyone "brother" or "father", but that might get confusing, too. Who is my father and who is my brother? These are difficult questions of the nuclear family and my nuclear family is just a bunch of guys in robes. No, far simpler to take a vow of silence. It would probably help me out just fine. I wouldn't have to remember names. I probably wouldn't have to memorize all the various prayers. I just need to learn the moves with my hands and possibly feet and I'm golden. It would be like line dancing in high school. I wouldn't imagine that conversation would be possible. No, if anything people might avoid speaking to me. And, I suppose, if someone were to speak to me at all, at any great length I would be in my right to smack them upside the head. They would want an explanation, but I'd be able to just hold my index finger to my closed mouth and nod. They'd be puzzled by all of this, but ultimately, through consultation with other monks, they will reach the conclusion that they were close to causing me to sin and break my vow of silence. They would feel ashamed then, and I would have a silent laugh. Yes, a monk's life could be just the ticket.

Looking around Sparks this midday there is far too much to make a man think of sin. All the young professional women, wearing their tight business skirts and blouses, it gets the mind racing. I wonder what Isabelle Fontaine is wearing today in Toronto. I can see her wearing a pantsuit, but one that still shows her beautiful form. I think it must be tight at her butt and waist and a bit looser down the legs. It's a shame, though, I imagine, as she probably has a stunning set of legs. I wonder if she goes out on weekends and if she wears skirts and high heels. Her calves are probably well defined. I think she must do yoga on Tuesdays and Pilates on Thursdays. She'd wear jogging pants then, tight ones, of course, and a sports bra, her well-chiselled abdomen breathing the same air as her perfect mouth. This all sends me into a frenzy, or maybe it's the humid Ottawa air, but a sweat builds on my forehead.

I reach the front of the line and order a hot dog and pretzel. The street vendor asks me what I want on top. I tell him to put ketchup on the hot dog and a little mustard on the pretzel. He puts a lot of both on the hot dog and leaves the pretzel undressed. I sigh and pay the vendor. You can't ask a lot from a man who sells street meat, that's my motto. I sit in the shade, under an awning and eat the hot dog. My stomach thanks me now for filling its void, though I have my concerns that it may be displeased this afternoon.

"It Was The Best of Times, It Was The Worst of Times: Dickensian Observations in Hamburg"
(Blog post, May 14, 2011)

Swish-swish, I am cruising towards the northern city of Hamburg from Berlin. A Google maps search tells me that it would take about three hours to drive, but on Deutsche Bahn's Intercity Express service, it takes only half that. As a man with a first class rail pass I have the privilege of sitting in a very large seat. It's an island unto itself, without anybody next to me, only an aisle. The seat reclines back, and I am swept back into blissful comfort. I almost wish that the train ride were longer for me to fully appreciate it. Like most forms of travel these days, riding first class doesn't entitle you to a whole lot, especially on such a short journey, but I enjoy the free bag of chocolate malted balls (like Maltesers, but not materially enough like Maltesers to cause branding issues).

**

Arriving in Hamburg, I remember the last time I was there, five years ago, as a short stop on the way to Copenhagen. It had been a Sunday and a quite awful one at that. There weren't many things going on then, and I am excited to see what the city has to offer me as I will be there all day Friday, overnight, and back to Berlin only at dinner time on Saturday. Please, please me, I think to myself. Show me what you have to offer.

I've come with one purpose: to see the Manic Street Preachers in concert. Everything else is secondary. In fact, it was so secondary that I didn't really look into accommodations until earlier in the week. I discovered that for fifty euros I could stay at an average hostel. For thirty, I could stay at an absolute dive.

I thought about these options and decided against either. For tonight, I am on a mission of fun. I will commit myself to just riding the wave of the evening, from the concert and onwards, and see where it takes me. I've done a few late nights in Europe and the prospect of partying until the daylight does not phase me. In fact, I think about how far thirty to fifty euros can go at three euros per beer. Who needs to pay for a bed that won't be slept in? The main train station (Hamburg Hbf) has 24-hour lockers that I can throw my stuff in, so I can move unencumbered.

**

I wander the streets and see much of what I saw last time. It's a pretty enough city, with cafes and galleries, and a nice area by the water, which I'm told is a lake, but find hard to believe because it appears to be a very square entity that juts into the centre of town. Like Berlin, there are lots of vendors selling currywurst mit pommes frites und eis (ice cream). In front of the city hall is a nice little square, where like most nice little squares in Europe, pigeons come to poop, people come to hover, and street performers come to be ignored.

**

I'm at the Markthalle, the venue for the evening. I've climbed stairs, shown my ticket, climbed more stairs, shown my ticket again, and reached a roadblock. A scruff biker type gives me the pat down. I apparently pass inspection and am sent forward to the actual entrance, which is across a rooftop gangway, where I show my ticket again. I read the sign clearly stating in about six languages that absolutely under no circumstances are cameras permitted and if found will be punishable by expulsion. I gulp a deep gulp remembering that in the front left pocket of my jeans is the Samsung ST90 that I've been taking all these lovely pictures with. It's funny, in a way, because I remember the pat down included a very particular slow down when my biker friend got to the pockets. He definitely touched the camera, the outline and the face of it, through denim, of course. He must have thought it was a mobile phone and moved on. I had bought the camera mostly because of the fact it was very slim, so in this case it proved its worth. I decide to play it cool and discretely slide the camera into my coat pocket (hiding the contraband as I should) and check my coat. I feel pretty proud of the fact that the offending item is safely stored until I leave the club.

The Markthalle (or "Marxhalle" as the clever signs inside read) is divided into three rooms. The first room you enter is the main bar area, with appropriately a bar, some tall counters and stools and not much else. At one end is another room, which based on the amount of smoke building up behind glass and the absence of smoke anywhere else in the club, makes me assume is probably for smokers. At the other end are some doors. Through the other side of the doors is the actual concert hall. It is not big, with room for 500 sane people or 1,000 otherwise inclined individuals. The hall has no seats, except for at the very back, in a sort of balcony area. However, in a rather clever design, the standing room floor is built in a series of half-circle tiers, so that those at the front and centre are lower than those at the back and sides. I find a spot that I judge to be pretty awesome, as it is right at the front of the hall, along a sidewall, with a raised view of everything. I'm fifteen feet from the microphone at stage centre and I'm leaning against a wall. Very nice! I can see that the only disadvantage of the spot is that I can't see where Sean Moore, the drummer for the Manics, will be playing, but I'll have a spectacular view of James Dean Bradfield (singer and lead guitarist) and the flamboyant Nicky Wire (bass). Sorry Sean, I think to myself.

The opening band is called the Joy Formidable and they are a cool group of late-20, early-30 somethings. They look exactly like every indie rock band you can imagine, with the cute blond female lead singer/guitarist (like a smaller Karen O.) and guys wearing plaid and skinny jeans. I hadn't heard their music before, so I was pleasantly surprised when I did. The first thing that came to mind, and it might have been due to the song and not necessarily the entirety of their set, but the Joy Formidable sounded a bit like Veruca Salt. Does anyone remember them? I saw them as the opening act for Bush (or Bush-x as they were called then) when I was 12. I also got a bit of a Metric vibe, but only if Metric were darker and angrier. The band is charming and has the crowd appreciating everything (rare for opening bands, so I am impressed with Hamburg already). They tell us that it's a big pleasure to be opening for the MSP (obviously), and that they remember being teenagers in northern Wales listening to them and it's a thrill to be there today.

Same with me. Except for the northern Wales part. The point is that I remember the Manic Street Preachers being a huge part of my teenage years, and they've continued to be. I remember the first time I heard the song "If You Tolerate This (Your Children Will Be Next)". I might have been thirteen and it was on the radio (CFOX 99.3 in Vancouver) loop every two hours. I'd listen to the radio all day just to hear the loop come around and hear that song again and again and again. I don't know of any other song that I've heard on a radio that made me do that before or after (and to be fair I've long stopped listening to the radio) but there is something special about the song. There is something special about the band.

I have a handful of musical artists that I'm not ashamed to say I quite enjoy. They range from the singer-songwriters that I go to for melancholic emotional affinity (Damien Rice, Ray LaMontagne and Ryan Adams) to the quirky indie pop bands I secretly dance to when I clean my apartment (Camera Obscura, Belle & Sebastian and Peter Bjorn & John). Throw in a few others, like Fleet Foxes, the Black Keys, and the Arctic Monkeys, along with classics like the Beatles, the Clash, and the Smiths and you've almost got my core tastes. There are lots of others, of course, covering other genres and styles, but that's almost it.

Then there are the Manic Street Preachers, who stand
alone. I don't think they are the greatest band ever.
I won't argue with anyone over that. I won't argue that
they are one of the most influential bands or anything
else, either. I will say that they are my favourite. They
have produced a very large series of albums over
twenty-plus years that span genres. I won't say that
every song is a gem, or that I even like all of them. I will
say that some of them are masterpieces. I will argue that
some of their albums are, too. They challenge me.
I listen to the lyrics and I hear the music and
I experience their art. It's not something I throw on for a
laugh or in the background with friends around.
It's something that I listen to with my headphones or
when I'm alone. They ask questions. That may not mean
much to anyone, but I like it very much. I think they are
far more intelligent than can usually be given credit to
rock bands. They ask questions about our understanding
of life, love, history, religion, politics, war, art, and death.
When I listen to them, I am forced to think of these
questions, too. The most challenging thing, I suppose,
is that there are always fewer answers than questions.

But tonight is not one of those times to ask questions.
It's a time to breathe in the same air as the Manics and
to just enjoy the music. The smoke machine starts and
they come on stage. I am here. This is happening.
Later we can ask whatever questions we want about the
meaning and purpose of life, but for the next ninety
minutes there is only one thing in my life and it is perfect.
So many people here all going through the same
thoughts and feelings as me. When James asks us to
sing along, we sing along loudly. It's brilliant. The one
time in my life when I can actually remember every lyric
when it's needed. Songs from every era are played.
I can only smile. This is glorious.

**

The concert is over and I decide to follow the crowd to
find the nightlife. But first, a minor pit stop at the coat
check. Half an hour later, and we're off.

Following the crowd down the street I notice that they've led me to the train station. No! You were supposed to take me to the nightclubs and dance halls, not retreat back to your suburbs!

**

I'm down by the lake and there is a restaurant with an outdoor patio that's open. It's almost one, so I'm glad just to find something open. Hamburg has let me down again. I order a beer and sit and ponder what I'm going to do for the rest of the night. Can I honestly sit outside at this near empty restaurant forever?

No. Evidently, I cannot. It's quarter to two and my waiter has asked me for my last call. I order a second beer and decide to milk it for what it's worth. I am in no rush. I watch the staff in the background packing up cabana furniture under the palm trees. Are they real? Surely palms can't survive in this climate. The staff scurry to and fro, rushing through their tasks, with an urgency that makes it clear that I probably shouldn't linger too long. I look around and there are only two other tables occupied. They are all finishing up. I sigh at the mice that I can see running around underneath the empty patio tables.

**

I decide that I am going to go for a walk around the heart of the city. Hopefully, if I have some luck, I'll find something worthwhile to join. I walk through the nice part of town and as nice parts of town usually are at two in the morning, it is absolutely deserted. There are bars here, all the lovely little places I walked by in the afternoon, locked and shut. One sushi restaurant has been converted into a karaoke bar, but looking through the windows I can see that it's really just a small group, possibly all family and the front door has a closed sign hung.

I head east and make a circle through a not so nice part of town. It's filled with sex shows and doner kebab shops. I walk down a couple blocks and hear dance music. Finally! I turn the corner, expecting the normal nightclub look. You know, a doorman and maybe a small line. Instead I see a sketchy looking dude smoking a cigarette. I look at the wall he is leaning against and it is not a nightclub. Where is this music coming from? I look up and there are big glass windows and a strobe light. I can clearly see into this "dancehall" that there are only a handful of people there and none of them seem to be dancing. This is awful. It couldn't possibly get worse.

It was maybe five minutes later when I was propositioned for sex. Now, I've seen Pretty Woman, and that basically sums up my entire knowledge of the sex trade. This woman was not Julia Roberts. I'll admit that I'm not Richard Gere, but that's really beside the point. This woman was by my guesses to be anywhere between thirty-five and seventy-two, depending on where she stood in the shadows of the lamp standards. I barked back quickly the word "no" in as many languages as I could remember. I decided that I better get a doner kebab.

On my way back to a shop that I had seen on my way to the sketchy dancehall, a genuinely cute prostitute (if I can make that judgment) stood, doing what can only be described as negotiating. She was entertaining the possibility of fulfilling whatever requests it was that the three British louts, likely over for the weekend on a stag party, could come up with. I heard some pleasant laughter on her part and boorish chuckles from the louts. Numbers were being tossed around. I carried on walking.

I sat at the sidewalk picnic table and looked at the beef doner. I looked up and saw the doors to a sex show. People came and went. A young couple, laughing, popped their heads in. Shortly thereafter they came out with the man frowning and the woman smiling playfully. Further down the street I could still see that old haggard woman waiting for someone to love her. The young cute prostitute and the Brits had disappeared. I ate the doner.

After being propositioned for money for sex, I was taken aback a bit by a voice asking for a very small sum of change. It was a beggar. I said sorry, but I didn't have any change. It was the truth. I had thirty euros in my wallet and had spent the last coins I had on the doner. I said no, sorry. I felt awful, as I usually do when I am asked by beggars (a nearly daily occurrence for me no matter what city I'm in). In a rather sad, though touching moment, the shop assistant popped out with a small bag that he handed to the beggar, whom he seemed to know by name. It was just a bit of food, but I could tell that the beggar appreciated it. He said something to the shop assistant and a small piece of baklava was thrown in, as well.

It was only two thirty and I was already done with Hamburg. I cursed my train reservation at six pm. That was foolish planning. I suppose I had thought that I should want to maximize my short time in the city. Foolish! You're now at two strikes, Hamburg. I'll come back here again in another five years and you'll have your last chance at redemption!

I turn down a street and start walking with no real intention. A crowd of young people come bouncing down the street, laughing and holding bottles of beer in their hands. I smile, thinking that I've found the way to or from a party. A pretty girl, wearing a long tight top over tights (the way pretty girls do), spoke to me. I smiled, and apologised in my limited German. I said I spoke English. She smiled a big wide smile and in broken English asked me if I wanted to join them. I was delighted. A friendly group of people, finally, inviting me to join in their partying. That would be perfect. I said sure. She said it would be fun; I could even have sex with her and everything. I thought it was just my luck that I was being whisked away out of the blue with a fun group of people and the pretty girl was already making advances (a bit forward, but this is Europe, right?). I pointed at her and asked dumbly, "with you?" She nodded and smiled. She then told me that they were all going to a room (there were three girls and another dude). I realised, though a bit late, that this was just another proposition. It was an interesting and baffling one, but a proposition nonetheless. She said that if I could chip in fifty euros it would be nice and the sex would be fun, too. I'm not a puritan by any means, but that's one line that I'll never cross. I did what anyone ought to do when confronted by people that only want you for your money; I told the pretty girl that I didn't have any money. None at all. Her smile disappeared. I felt vindicated that I was correct in this assessment, though I also felt a little disappointed that it wasn't my dashing good looks that caused a stranger to offer sex.

I continue down the street and see that I've found an area that if it isn't the "official" red light district, certainly had a lot of red lights. Sex bars lined the street. I peer through the windows and sadly laugh that even these are empty on a late Friday night (or early Saturday morning).

**

I'm sitting in the train station because it is warmish and the lights are on. It's three in the morning and I feel as low as I've ever felt before. Maybe lower in absolute terms, as I don't think I had ever felt as high as I did during the concert. Falling from such great heights to these depths takes a lot out of a man. I've found a small stairway that has a locked gate across the top. I sit on the steps, slightly out of the way of the passing traffic. People come and go, as you might expect at a major train station. I have no idea where they are coming and going from, though.

There are three teenagers, no older than fifteen, walking up to the passersby and asking for change. They see no success. They play a three-person game of rock-paper-scissors and the loser asks the next passerby for twenty cents. Still no success. I watch them and wonder what

they are doing at the Hamburg Hbf at this hour.
They aren't dressed poorly like a "typical" beggar and
just look like a group of kids that forgot to put aside a bit
of cash for the return train ride.

A drunk stumbles down the corridor, eyes closed.
His feet slide along the ground slowly, moving in short
strides. It is taking him several minutes to walk past me.
He turns, blindly, and starts stutter-stepping his way
towards my perch on the steps. I don't know what to do,
so I sit and watch. He makes it to the bottom step, eyes
still closed, and falls down across the stairs. His head
lands not more than a foot from me and I can see that it
has gashes and abrasions from bumping into things,
presumably more stairs and walls. I sigh and leave the
man to sleep.

**

The McDonalds restaurant in the station is packed with
people, all wearing their finest dance clothes. Where did
they come from? Which great party did I miss? I feel so
disconnected from everything. German words and
German laughter surround me. Here I am just this fool
who came for a concert, experienced the best concert of
his life and has to deal with the fallout of not knowing
what to do in life Post-Manics. I sip a coffee.

**

Time to get out. I just need to leave. I take my rail pass
and jump onto the first train that I can get back to Berlin.
It is packed and a quick glance at the displays above the
seats indicate that everything is reserved. I feel
immediately defeated and know that I will likely have to
try another train.

**

I sit and watch the sunrise and realise that I survived it
all. In a moment of clarity I just accept that it was a rotten
night, but not to think much more of it than that. This trip
has been great overall, with a few rough patches,

but I need to focus on the positive and push through.
There are too many people that would love to be where I
am to feel awful.

**

Having decided to make the most of my remaining time
in Hamburg, I head to the Hamburg Kunsthalle
(art gallery) and spend four hours absorbing everything.
It is like a reset button to my soul.

**

I get on the train and ride back to Berlin with nothing on
my mind but sleep.

Excerpt from

"With Respects to Our Glorious Soviet Past"

(Blog post, May 16, 2011)

Berlin is this strange beast that has changed so much and yet stayed so much the same over time. It's roughly the same size in population now (3.8 million) as it was when central Berlin and the surrounding areas were amalgamated into a city a hundred years ago. Over that span of time there have been many different rulers and governments. There was the Prussian Kaiser who ruled from Sansoucci in nearby Potsdam, the Weimar Republic, the rise of Hitler and the Nazis, post-war occupation by the Allied powers, the divided city and country of the Cold War, and finally reunification. Walking through the streets it isn't hard to see the touches that each era has left. Arguably the largest impact has been left by the Soviets and their East German comrades (or puppets, as it goes).

Ask anyone about Berlin and they'll mention the Wall. It has this ominous sound to it and by all accounts it was a dehumanising piece of architecture. From 1961 to 1989 a city and its people were divided. The Iron Curtain was for most purposes a rather abstract line that cut Europe in half, with the democratic West on one side and the communist East on the other. In Berlin it took on a very real and not at all abstract form. In the just over a decade between the liberation of Berlin from the Nazis by the Soviets and the erection of Wall, 2.5 million East Germans fled to the West. The Soviet lifestyle was hardly liberating. To stem the flow of people (workers needed in a command economy), the Wall was put in place, with only one entry, the infamous Checkpoint Charlie. Attached to the Wall were one hundred watchtowers. Alongside the Wall were "dead zones", open areas not to be trespassed.

136 East Berliners who tried to flee were shot in the dead zones. For the most part, almost the entire Wall is gone. It was torn down in rapturous celebration in November 1989. But there are still reminders everywhere. It becomes an exercise in attention, but it is well worth it. Those who forget our past are destined to repeat history.

The flat that I am renting is actually in the former West Berlin, but just a stone's throw from where the Wall existed for twenty-eight years. The route of my run that I wrote about a while back, the one straight to the Reichstag and back, actually follows where the Wall used to be. Looking down at the ground you can see in the path two rows of brick. Every now and then, maybe every couple of hundred metres you can look down and read the engravings that read "Berliner Mauer 1961-1989". When I wrote that the area by the Spree I ran in had a bit of nature and industry, I had no idea that the nature that existed there was actually largely the result of thirty years of neglect. I had been running along a former part of the dead zone. Those watchtowers? Yep, I had been running by one of the remaining three that still stand all along.

I went to Checkpoint Charlie, but for the most part it's been incorporated into the street. Regular traffic flows right through now. There is a museum, of course, practically everything in Berlin is a museum, and there are some informative historical timelines along a fence (the inside is a beach beer garden called Charlie's), but mostly the Checkpoint is just an excuse for vendors to hock fake Soviet hats.

"A Confession"
(May 16, 2011)

"Open the door."

Ryan only heard silence on the other side.

"Please, Rebecca, I know you are home. I know you can hear me. I need you to open the door. I can explain everything. It was all just a big misunderstanding. Please, just open the door."

Still no sound came from the other side. He couldn't hear footsteps coming to open the door. He heard no uneasy ruffling of items by the front door. Silence, pure and simple, was all that he could hear. It was the absence of any sound. It was the absence of any confirmation of his pleas. He needed to say what he had thought about on the ride there. It was an excruciating ride into downtown. He hated the Expo line. It lacked the sophistication of the Canada line and wasn't a historical route like one finds in London or New York. It was just a dated, dirty line that connected Zones 1 and 2. Ryan had thought it was a smart idea to live in North Delta to save money on rent, but he ended up spending the difference in transit fares and cab rides, so often was he in the West End. Once again he found himself riding the SkyTrain to see her. It was hard enough to clear his mind and think of the things he needed to say to Rebecca without having to drown out the stupid Goth kids and the drunken louts. It was also a game night and the train was packed with people wearing the orange, white, silver and black of the Lions. At Stadium they all alighted and it was just Ryan with his thoughts. He even stayed on the train all the way to Waterfront when Burrard was closer to Rebecca's apartment, using the extra few minutes to gather those last few words he needed. Walking up Howe Street he knew that this was one of those pivotal moments, you know the kind of event that can forever shift a life.

Ryan had felt that way only a couple of times before in his short life but knew it for certain when it was happening.

"I love you, Rebecca. You must know that. I know I've never said it before, but it's true. I love you with everything in my heart. I want you to know that. I know that you must. You must know that. You are everything to me and I only want to be with you. I love you and want to spend forever with you. I've said it. It's out there. I'm not just saying it now, because of what happened. I really mean it. It's a horrible circumstance for this to be the time and the place for me to say it, but it must be said. If you're to listen to me and trust me, you must know how I feel. I love you, Rebecca. I just want you to open the door, but if you won't do that, I can't blame you. You can just sit there and listen. Listen, please, listen to what I have to say, because it can all be explained. Everything is just one big misunderstanding. It isn't like you think it is. I don't want you to think otherwise, so let me tell you what happened, from the beginning, sparing no detail. After that, I hope that you'll understand what happened. I hope that I can clear up that horrible misunderstanding. You must know that I love you and I wouldn't ever do something to try and hurt you. You must know that, Rebecca. It didn't happen that way at all. I'd ask you to tell me you understand, but I know that you won't speak a word to me. It's not hard for me to understand where you are coming from, so I'll not ask. I'll just sit here on this side of the door and you can sit there on the other and listen to the man that loves you tell you what happened. Is that okay?"

Ryan continued to hear only silence.

"I'll take it that it is okay, and even if it isn't, I need to say it. It started on Monday evening, well that is to say that the beginning of this story begins on Monday. The event, what you saw, that didn't start then. Let me correct that, I am muddling my words. I shouldn't say that it began or started or ended or anything like that. It wasn't an ongoing event. It happened just then, just when you saw

it. That is it. It was a one-off event and even then a very
brief and awkward interaction that was the result of a
horrible misunderstanding. It wasn't meant to happen.
I certainly didn't mean for it to occur. It just did.
You know? No, of course you don't know. You shouldn't
know. It was just one of those things that you can't
foresee and yet all the signs led up to it, but I was just
blind to see it. I'm often like that, you know that about
me, I can be absolutely clueless sometimes. I remember
that one time down at Kits Beach when we were leaving
and you gave me that look like I should know what you
were looking at me for. Do you remember? I had no idea
what that look was about. I hadn't even seen that couple.
I can't believe you noticed them and I didn't. I can't
believe that they did that there, open on the beach for all
the world to see. Well, not all the world, as I obviously
didn't see. But that's just my point! I'm clueless and that
is why these things happen that I just don't notice.
I miss signs all the time. Not just metaphorical ones
either, but I am always missing real, physical signs, too.
I sometimes miss my stop on the SkyTrain and I need to
get off and ride back one station. It's embarrassing, but
that's part of who I am. I won't make apologies for every
little thing like that that I do, but I am here to tell you that
what you saw, what you witnessed was one thing
I should have seen coming and I should have put the
brakes to it long before. I can be clueless sometimes,
but there are times when I obviously need to get myself
in order. I need to know about certain things, especially
when people's hearts are involved. I don't want to hurt
anyone, I really don't. You know that I really love you
and the last thing I'd want to do is cause you pain.
You remember how awful I felt when you went away that
week, to the conference in Edmonton and I took care of
your aquarium? I didn't mean to kill your fish, I really
didn't. I thought I had fed them the right amount.
I swear I checked the pH levels every day, twice I think,
and everything seemed fine. I don't know what
happened, but the day you were to return I came to your
apartment to find all six of those Tetras floating upside
down. I felt as bad as a person could. At least I thought

so at the time. I feel worse now. I really do. I love you
Rebecca and I don't want you to be hurt. I can
understand if you are mad, but I want you to know the
truth of what happened so that you might forgive me and
we can move forward. I need you in my life and I would
hope that you would want me in yours. I know that you
don't need me. Of course you don't need me. You don't
deserve me either. I get that. You can do so much better
than me, but I am a fool and I know that I could never do
better than you. I love you so much and I want to be with
you until the end of time itself. It's true. I've thought
about that many times. I know I've never said anything
until now. I didn't want to overwhelm you. I just wanted
things to happen on their own, organically and such and
not pressure you. I thought if I ever was foolish enough
to say those words, you might not say them back to me.
How sad is that, Rebecca? A man, who is madly in love
with a woman, truly loves her, and he isn't able to say it.
That is the definition of sadness, I should think.
No, I really do love you and at this point I don't care if
that overwhelms you and I don't fear that you won't say it
back to me. I fear that you should never speak to me
again and that is far scarier than you not saying
a particular three or four words. I think at this point
I could live the rest of my life without hearing that you
love me if it meant that I could wake up next to you.
Would you like that? Would you consider liking me
enough to wake up next to me everyday? You wouldn't
even have to fully love me. You'd know that I love you
and that is something. What am I saying? I shouldn't be
asking you to spend the rest of your life with me.
Not like this, not right now. I should only ask for your
forgiveness, and hope that I can see you again.
We can take it day by day. That should be enough for
me. I'm a fool, I've mentioned that, Rebecca, and surely
for all this time that you've known me you've known that
about me, too. I don't mean to cause harm, but
sometimes foolish as I am, it just happens.
Do you remember when your father asked you about his
cigars? Remember, he wanted to know what happened
to that one from the box at the cabin?

You said you had no idea what happened to it, that we didn't touch them when we were up there. You said that we don't even smoke so what would we have to do with his cigars. Oh, I felt awful and I should have told you then, but I know what happened to his cigar. I didn't mean to. I really didn't. I just took it out of the box to smell it. I'd never seen a real Cuban before. I just wanted to give it a whiff, just to see what it smelled like. You know? Sometimes I do the same at people's homes, in their washrooms when they've got interesting soaps and candles. It's strange, I know, but it's usually harmless. Well, I had his cigar up to my nose, in the bathroom and I was giving it a sniff when you knocked on the door. It startled me and I dropped the cigar. I dropped it right into the toilet. Obviously I wasn't going to fish it out. That would be awful on so many levels. I wouldn't want to reach in the toilet bowl and I wouldn't wish for anyone to ever have to smoke a cigar that's been in the toilet. So I let it sit there. It was a big one and there wasn't much water, but I wanted to make sure that I could flush it. I had to wait until it looked soggy enough to go. I think I sat in there for twenty minutes. I told you I had a stomach thing. I didn't want anyone to see. I'm ashamed of it now and I feel awful for what you said to your father. I don't know if he believed you and I feel as though he's never liked me and his suspicions about the cigar only made it worse, as if somehow I had corrupted his daughter. But this isn't about that. No, I do feel some relief telling you about that cigar. Maybe this is just what we needed to get everything out in the open. We can start fresh and move on. I'd like that, I really would. You know that you mean the world to me and I will do whatever it takes to win back your trust. While we are at it, I should probably tell you that I did, in fact, read your diary a couple times. I didn't want to, I know that is personal and I should have respected that, but you know sometimes curiosity can make people do rash things. The first time was early, maybe after we had been dating for a month or so. I was insecure and I wanted to know what you thought of me. You've never been talkative. Ha! I mean, look at right now for example you aren't saying a thing. But, no, I shouldn't joke. I want to be honest and straightforward with you. I waited until you hopped in the shower that day and I grabbed your diary and flipped it open. I wish I hadn't. It's not that I found anything bad, but the opposite. Reading such lovely words about myself just filled my ego up. It can be addicting, actually. So, a couple times along the way, I've occasionally opened up your diary to feel better about myself, hoping to read something nice. Most of the time it worked. A couple of times, though, I think I found things I ought not to know. Things that probably were better kept secret. I suppose that's why you wrote them in a diary. I am really sorry about that and I promise from now on to not read your diary. I also think, for the health of our relationship, you ought to change your email password. I don't want to have that power or privilege. It would help if you signed out each time you were done on my computer, too. Clear the history and the cookies as well. I don't want to go on and see what you've been up to. I don't want to be nosy, but sometimes you make it too easy. Wow, that felt good to say. I am sorry about all that, but it's for the best, right? Right, of course, you still aren't speaking to me. I've been on a tangent or two and I still need to get to what happened. It started on Monday and I was completely unaware. Heather had been helping me set up the front window at the shop that evening, after closing. There was the big sale on Tuesday, you remember that? Yes, of course you do, you bought that pashmina for your mom, and I think a skirt or a dress for yourself. Anyways, on Monday evening, we were setting up the window display and Heather said something to me that I must have completely misread. She was wondering what sort of thing a guy would want from the sale. I said I don't really know, but there are lots of interesting items that could work. I said it depended on what type of guy she was looking at getting the gift for. She said she was thinking of getting something nice for a guy she's liked for quite sometime. I said that was a bit easier at narrowing it down. We took a break from the window display and I walked her over to the men's section and we took a

look at the accessories. There were a lot of nice wallets, belts, wristbands, sunglasses and so on that I thought would be a thoughtful gift. She asked my opinion on which I thought was best. I pointed out the messenger bag that I had seen arrive that morning. It was this gorgeous thing, a brown canvas bag with leather.
I said that was probably the nicest thing a fellow could receive. She thanked me and I helped her wrap it up. Anyways, that was the last shift that Heather worked with me until last night. She has classes at Kwantlen during the week so for the most part she usually works weekends. That's not important, really, for this story, but it helps explain why I should have paid more attention on Monday. Because last night, at the end of our shift, as we were just closing up the shop, Heather came to me with a gift. I was confused, because I am a fool, and didn't notice any of the signs leading up to it. I opened up the package and saw the very same messenger bag that I had picked out. Heather told me that she had liked me for sometime and that she wanted to go out with me. Before I could respond she leaned in and planted a kiss right on my lips. It was at that moment that you arrived to meet me for all-you-can-eat sushi. In all the minutes of the day, you arrived at the worst possible moment.
You saw us, locked in lips and you turned away and ran. I heard your footsteps and I ran after you, but you got in that cab and drove away. I called you, but you wouldn't answer. I went back to the store and I told Heather everything. I told her that I already had a girlfriend.
I told her that I loved you, Rebecca. I told her that I didn't realise that she had feelings for me. I felt gutted.
I felt like that moment might have ruined my life.
She apologised and I think she was very embarrassed by her own declaration. She said she would return the bag at once. It wouldn't be right for me to have it.
I agreed, even if it was a lovely bag. She said something about just being a foolish girl. I told her not to worry, life is full of foolish moments. I said that, but I knew that it was more important to me than just a foolish mistake. I tried calling you all last night, but you wouldn't answer. I didn't leave many messages. Maybe just a couple.

They were short, weren't they? Anyways, I had to work today, so I couldn't come over until now. Heather called in sick. She wasn't there today, in case you were concerned. I wouldn't be concerned. I don't think she is going to make any crazy advances on me again.
I just wanted to let you know all about it. I wanted you to hear the truth. I may have said some things that I didn't mean to, like your diary and the cigar, but it's out there now. I hope you can forgive me and we can move on.
I love you. You've now heard me say it, like, a million times, even though I've never said it to you before today. Maybe it took something crazy like this to make me say it, but it's out there. I've held your ear for long enough. You obviously don't want to speak to me, so I'll go now. I hope that you'll talk to me soon. I can't bear to think of a life without you, Rebecca. Goodbye."

Ryan stood up and looked one last time at the door. He heard silence. There was no last rush of footsteps to open the door. He sighed and walked down the hallway to the elevator. He pressed the down button and watched the light above the door as it made its way from the ground level up to the twenty-first floor. The door opened and facing Ryan was Rebecca.

"Rebecca!"

"Ryan, what are you doing here?"

"I came to tell you everything, about last night, about what you thought you saw."

"Oh, that's alright, Ryan. I spoke to Heather today."

"You did?"

"Yes. She called me up and asked to meet me for coffee. She wanted to clear the air and she told me the whole story. She actually seems like a very nice girl and didn't know that you were seeing anyone."

"Oh."

"So, you're not mad with me?"

"Nope, it was all just a big misunderstanding. I've been trying to call you all day. Did you have your phone on you?"

"Yeah, I think so."

Ryan reached into his pocket and pulled out his mobile. He pressed the call button to light up the screen but nothing happened.

"Shit, I think it's dead."

"I'm not surprised. You called me like fifty times last night."

Rebecca smiled and put her arms around Ryan's neck.

"You know, Ryan, I've never said it, but I'll say it now: I love you."

Excerpt from
"Delicate Arms"
(Unpublished novel)

It was a sea of chaos wrapped in houndstooth. I stood at
the bottom of Portobello Road and looking up could see
not an inch of empty ground between where I was and
the top of the hill, as it curved to the left. The soft pastels
of the buildings provided little comfort to me the
trembling ant, as I wanted to make my way through the
stampede. One shop was draped in a sunflower yellow,
followed by a turquoise blue, and a sea foam green.
It was all just so goddamned cute. Ominously cute,
though, as I was trying to make my way through the
street. Had everyone arrived straight from Heathrow with
me? Where could a man breathe in London?
Everywhere I went I seemed to be swallowed up in a
ruckus, in a fuss, in a storm of people cycloning their
way to have some biscuits or scones. Benevolent acts
became shrouded with harrowing danger. I had already
found myself walking on the wrong side of the sidewalk,
causing both impoliteness and near collisions. Every
Nigel and Clive seemed to take umbrage with me.
I didn't want to find out if fisticuffs come out quickly in
this part of town. That's just it, too! For all I can tell I had
just been in the West End, the nice part of town. If this is
what the posh folks act like in the toney boroughs like
Kensington and Chelsea, what help would I have in the
rough and tumble cockney East?

I know one thing; I shall try and avoid wearing any
specific football colours that might cause a fuss. I look
down at myself and see that I am wearing a conspicuous
olive green jacket. That should do just fine. As far as my
limited knowledge of London soccer teams go, I don't
think any of the major ones wear subdued greens.
My t-shirt underneath is just a plain grey, without any
logos. I might do okay. I think I've avoided accidentally

aligning myself with Fulham, Chelsea, Arsenal, West Ham, Tottenham or some of the smaller clubs I know about. The last thing I want to do is run into some skinhead punks who get upset that I'm wearing a generic five-dollar t-shirt of a primary colour that just so happens to match one of the twelve colours their rival club wears. I don't think that I would handle that situation very well at all. I don't know if I'd make it worse by saying that I don't follow football. Would that offend them? It's the world's game! Besides, in any case I know a little. I know enough not to call it soccer, even though that word originates in England. Somehow it's just the colonies that have kept its usage. It was refreshing for me to watch the World Cup in South Africa and hear other people beyond North Americans call it that. Of course, the Aussies also call it soccer, but they do it in the way only Australians can, naming their national team the Socceroos. It's both delightful and stupid. The point is that I wouldn't want to upset a skinhead punk by calling the sport he loves a name he detests. Or maybe it would help me prove my innocence in wearing a blank t-shirt with no affiliation to anyone and not a single FA logo on it. Yes, I am just a dumb Canadian. I have no idea about soccer. Please don't hurt me. That would do the trick. Of course, then, being proper hosts the skinhead punks would invite me for a pint. You must have a pint with us, our Canuck friend, you must. We'd enter some dingy pub named after two incongruous things, like the Stag & Tower, the Rose & Yacht, the Hound & Castle, and so on. A large bloke would tend bar, and he'd most certainly be named something like Terry. The skinhead punks would introduce themselves and reveal that beneath the grim exterior lies a very similarly grim interior.

"Y'alright, mate?"

"Yes, thank you, I am quite fine."

"Have you been in London for long?"

"I just arrived today."

"You here to see Ben and that?"

"Big Ben? Yes, I suppose that is part of any tourist's trip, right?"

"Yeah, I never seen the appeal, meself. It's just a big clock, innit?"

"Well, actually, I've heard that Ben is actually the name of the bell, and not the actual clock or tower."

"Shut it, you muppet."

I would take a sip of whatever pint they've found for me. It would be something incredibly cheap and they'd call it a session beer. I'd learn that they call them that because they are meant to be drunk in binge sessions.
How charming it all was here in the epicentre of the Anglophone world.

"So, Leon, can you tell me what you would recommend seeing?"

"Naw, it's all shit, mate. You've just got mugged off."

"I don't know half of what you are saying."

"I said it's a complete waste that you've spent all that bread to come here. London is a hole. You could have gone somewhere nice like Spain."

"Oh, I've been to Spain. I quite liked it. Barcelona is really interesting. It seems to have a bit of everything. There's the history, obviously all the civil war stuff, and then the art and architecture is really interesting."

"And them beaches. They've got them topless beaches, innit?"

"Yes, I remember that they did, indeed, have topless beaches. But, I'll tell you something, Leon, it was almost too much. You know?"

"I don't. Go on then."

"I stood there on the edge of the Mediterranean and I'm looking out at thousands of bronzed women standing there in all of their glory and it was too much. You can't stare, of course, and it becomes nearly impossible not to have your view obstructed by a naked breast. If I can't stare, where am I to rest my eyes? It was like the Ark of the Covenant."

"The what?"

"From the Bible, the Ark of the Covenant."

"Is that the thing with all the animals and such?"

"It was basically a box that contained God Himself and if you were to look upon the inside of it, the power of His Holiness would actually melt your face."

"Like in Indiana Jones?"

"Yes, actually, that is correct. That's supposed to be the very same Ark."

"So, you couldn't stare at all them beautiful titties because your face would melt off?"

"Something like that, yeah."

But I wasn't in that pub, the Thorn & Whistle, or whatever it was, and there was no Leon, the skinhead punk. I was still at the bottom of Portobello Road and I had made the mistake of coming on a busy weekend market day. There were stalls everywhere holding knick-knacks and curios. The shops were filled with sardined people. The street side cafes had given up on trying to serve people at their outdoor tables; such was the volume of the traffic. Crammed between the stalls and the people and the parked cars and the people and the stalls and the people and under the awnings of the shops were more people. It didn't end. I could not see anything but the tops of heads. Good luck finding an I. Cafieri in this traffic.

**

After slowly weaving my way to the top of Portobello
Road, I've reached a bit of breathing space. I feel a bit of
a sense of accomplishment in escaping that
claustrophobic nightmare. I also feel a bit of emptiness.
I never really got to see what I had set out to find.
I was hoping to find, sitting on the ground in a cheap
wood frame a hand-painted forest scene, with a river
and a cottage. I saw nothing of the sort. I saw all kinds of
old silverware and surplus military equipment.
There were bone china and ivory carvings. I saw stacks
of old LP records. Vinyl fascinates me, because it seems
to exist in a strange anachronistic way, despite being
made obsolete several times, it just won't go away.
DJs still flip records and now many bands, not just the
quirky types, have put in the effort of releasing albums
on vinyl again. I don't know if it's because they've found
the one form that people might still pay for or because
they want to have some sort of physical archive that
confirms they do exist. That's the thing about the digital
age, everything is out there in the cloud, easy to find and
access, but probably just as easy to find and destroy.
I don't wish to see the day that everything on the internet
implodes. All that built up knowledge, lost forever.
It would be like the library of Alexandria. I sometimes
dream of a post-apocalyptic future when electricity is
scarce or absent. I could see people finding old vinyl
records of David Bowie and playing them on a
19th century wind-up phonograph in a strange double
anachronism. If that should ever come to pass, I might
want to buy one of the gas masks they are selling here.
That's the thing about the apocalypse; one could never
have too many gas masks.

Excerpt from
"Berlin: Just Go Already!"
(Blog post, June 1, 2011)

I left Berlin a week and a half ago and I can tell you that it earned a great place in my heart. Klaus Wowereit, mayor in 2003 said it best, "Berlin is poor, but sexy." I had spent only three days there on my first trip when backpacking through Europe in 2006 and could instantly tell that I had unfinished business. Having spent three and a half weeks there this year, I feel the same. I guess next time it has to be for three months or longer...

**

Berlin is a huge city with unbelievable amounts of history and character. The best way to describe the city to someone who hasn't been is that Berlin is a place for all. All kinds of people with all kinds of interests and tastes WILL find something in Berlin. I don't say that without believing it. I can honestly understand how some people may not enjoy other great cities like New York or London (though I really do). Berlin is different. It honestly has twenty-four hours of entertainment – and best still, it does it without pretence. That's right, Berlin is open to all. It is a centre for fashion, music, art and other forms of culture, and yet, it is still very much a city that wears blue jeans. There are more nightclubs where you don't need to worry about how you dress than the ones that you do. It is pretty much the opposite of most cities in that regard. Wrinkled t-shirt and running shoes? No problem.

On my last Friday night in the city, I went to Magnet Club in Kreuzberg and had a great time. It was "late" by Canadian standards when I arrived, but I was there in time to see a great up and coming indie artist, Twin Shadow. Great show! Twin Shadow (George Lewis, Jr.) is an artist that mixes 80s new wave with some

R&B sensibilities. I had never heard of him before, but was glad to be won over by a great performance in a small music hall, something that Magnet is known for. When that set was over, Karrera Klub, local DJs, took over and "spun" a bunch of fantastic indie rock and pop that kept the hipster kids dancing. That's right! Hipsters do, too, dance! It's not just sad swaying. Loved it. In my thick-rimmed glasses and Adidas Sambas, I only felt out of place by my lack of German vocabulary. But when the music playing, whether from Toronto, Montreal, New York, London, or Stockholm is in English, we all felt at home. Ever get chills down the back of your neck? Yeah, that happened when I heard one hundred Berliners singing the lyrics to Arcade Fire's "Ready to Start". So far from home, but not alone.

**

I guess, in conclusion, all I can say is Berlin, "Es war toll" and "Ich liebe dich".

Danke.

The Places Inbetween, Or,
Six Nights Without Prose

Excerpt from

"Prague: It's Kafka-esque! (maybe... I haven't read any of his works...)"

(Blog post, June 3, 2011)

After departing Berlin, I headed south through central Europe by train. Not really having much of a plan other than knowing I needed to be in Budapest on the 28th, I decided to spend two nights each in Prague, Vienna and Bratislava. What happens when you fly by the seat of your pants is that not surprisingly you arrive in places that you know absolutely nothing about.

Such was my arrival in Prague, or as the locals call it "Praha". I was immediately astonished to see the price of drinks at the train station. I had heard that Prague wasn't exactly the cheap destination it was fifteen years ago, but looking at the numbers on the board was giving me flashbacks to Copenhagen (which I will swear to anyone who will listen is the most expensive city in Europe). It was only when I got a closer look at the vendor's price board that I noticed that it wasn't in Euro at all. Thank goodness for that. I've spent a bit on things through my travels but I had no interest in anything that cost 35 euro, especially if I would just drink it right away. No, I found out that the Czechs still used their own currency (the koruna or crown). Finding the local bureau de change, I could make the conversion to Canadian dollars. $1 = 17k. Well, that was helpful. Apparently those drinks cost two dollars. Simple enough. I just hadn't planned to have to learn a new currency until I got to Hungary, so this was a bit of a surprise (like I said, I really didn't plan this leg of the trip too much).

As I stood in line at the bureau de change, someone offering a better deal on the exchange approached me.

I wasn't in the mood to negotiate with random people and ignored the comment about the commission. Sure enough, the bureau took its cut (which is common at train stations), but if I had waited until I was in central Prague, I could have exchanged for 0%. Little lessons you learn. C'est la vie. Or, as the Czechs might say: "to je život" (assuming Google translate didn't mangle that up).

Now the only reason I bring up the random person approaching me is that at that point, roughly six minutes and 300m from exiting my train they were probably the fourth person to approach me. I've got a big backpack covered in patches of countries I've visited so I look very much the tourist. In fact, I was hopping off the train at the platform when I almost nearly knocked a poor woman over. I don't know any Czech so I quickly spat out "sorry" in German and English (because as you might already know, we Canadians have a habit of apologising for bumping into other people, even if it's not our fault). The woman looked at me with alert eyes and in perfect English asked me if I had accommodations. I had barely left the train! I said yes, I did, and she wandered further down the platform. What a strange occurrence, I thought. I don't think I've ever seen anything like that. Now, in between that and getting to the bureau de change it happened a couple more times, only by random looking dudes. It was only after I had got my Czech money that I saw each of the people who had spoken to me, gathered together, talking to each other in a group. They had accommodations and money, all right. So strange. Later in my stay in Prague I heard from other travellers who had met people who had gone and stayed with that type of random arrangement, not understanding the exchange rate, and ended up spending $300/night to sleep in a guest bedroom! There was none of that for me. I'm all about finding the best bang for my buck, or crash for my cash, or something. I can't find anything clever with koruna.

I stayed at a really interesting hostel (St. Christopher's Inn at the Mosaic House), which was as high tech and eco-friendly a place as I had ever seen. It was practically brand new and had some wild features, such as rooms that regulate their temperature automatically based on body heat (which makes things awkward when you walk in on a couple, um, occupying a single bunk with the privacy curtain closed – which was the first thing I did upon arriving). The hostel was so much like a hotel, that it was filled with atypical hostellers – plenty of people in their forties and fifties (and the fellow in the bunk above me could definitely have been a university student during the Prague Spring of 1968). I even had an RFID pass card for my room, adding to the swank hotel vibe.

[Side note: when I went backpacking five years ago, most hostels were very much still youth hostels and had age limits. Some had minimum ages, from 16 or 18 or 21 and up. There were often commonly maximum age limits, up to 26 or 30, for example. This seems to have largely gone out of practice and most (though not all) hostels now seem to be generally open to all. As I'm now 26, I can see the pros to that… It also seems to me that hostels fill the price point that discount hotels used to occupy which have gone up in price.]

But you don't want to hear about my accommodations. You want to hear about Prague. I actually think you want to see Prague. Because, and this is no exaggeration, when I arrived in Prague I saw the prettiest city I've ever seen before (and I've seen a few). I spent my first afternoon wandering around, soaking in the architecture, the river, the hillside parks, and just generally enjoying the city. I felt a bit ashamed that I didn't know anything about the place, but if first impressions are key, then Praha

**

That evening I met up with a friend from university that I hadn't seen in years and their partner whom I had never met. We went out to dinner and had a traditional Czech meal. It was actually the first restaurant that I had really splurged on during my trip (trying to do this on the cheap), but I figured catching up with a friend was a great excuse. My meal was stuffed duck medallions, with cabbage and dumplings. It was delicious! A general rule for me at restaurants is that I try to get things that I wouldn't normally make at home (it's easier to forget the price). Well, I certainly have never made stuffed duck. To wash it down, we were drinking 1L glass mugs of Gambrinus beer. It should be said that 1L is a lot of beer. It should be said. It wasn't. In fact, I remember having more than one. Also delicious.

**

Three in the morning in Prague and everything is still buzzing. It was the Anti-Hamburg as far as I was concerned. The bar inside the hostel had long been closed and the group of us had been sent out to the front of the building to drink. A convenience store across the street was still open and the shopkeeper was very friendly. I had made acquaintances with another Canadian and it was just so nice to chat endlessly about bullshit and life and philosophy and art and hockey. We were drunk, what more could you want from me?

**

Hangovers seem to hurt more in foreign countries.

**

The spread of the all you can eat breakfast was pretty decent and I tried to eat whatever I could that would soak up the suffering that was going on in my throbbing skull. Just as I was about to grab seconds, a very cheery Englishman wearing a straw hat and a red t-shirt came bouncing through the room asking if anyone was coming on the free tour. I looked at the clock and saw that it was nearly 10:30, which rang a bell with me as my friends had mentioned something last night about a free walking tour in the morning. I decided to roll with it, and finished my breakfast. Hardly all I could eat, but I was impressed with myself for getting up at all. You're welcome, Prague. I guess I will see you.

**

The three-hour walking tour was a fantastic way to make the most of my short time in the city. For anyone who is travelling through Europe I highly recommend Sandeman's New Europe walking tours (apparently they are in a bunch of cities). I really didn't know much about Prague or the Czech Republic and I left that tour feeling like our guide had crammed as much information in an entertaining way as possible into my brain. The best part is that the tour is free and then you tip your guide what you rate their "performance" to be. I found the thing so good that I couldn't help but leave a good tip (not understanding the Czech currency also played a part). The midway stop for lunch was also welcome as I could grab a sandwich, drink some water and, of course, enjoy a beer (best way to cure a hangover?). I learned about the founding of the city, the various religious sects that had/have occupied it, all the Czech ingenuity (microwave ovens, anyone?), and Mozart's love for the city (he felt that Prague "got him"). Of course, it wouldn't be a tour of Prague without a mention of Franz Kafka, who goes down in history as an unsuccessful writer at the time of his death, and a great success afterwards. All due to his friend disobeying his wish to burn his writing after he dies. What an awful friend.

But the biggest part of the tour is the political history of the 20th century. Seeing places where the Nazis came in, where the city fought back at the end of the war, where the Soviets showed up to "liberate" (after the Nazis had left), where a student had self-immolated in protest to the Soviet rule in 1969, it was all very, very powerful. It was interesting to hear the perspective that to Czechs the Second World War didn't end for them until 1989, as they didn't gain their freedom until then.

**

Prague has a lot of absinthe shops. Bad idea.

Excerpt from

"Vienna: Highest Standard of Living,
Not So Bad For Visiting, Too!"
(Blog post, June 6, 2011)

Ahh, Vienna. How to begin to describe a city that consistently ranks among the highest in living standards in the world? Well, how about with that fact? Sure. That works.

Vienna to the English, Wien (pronounced "veen") to the locals, is an absolute delight. It was a place, much like Prague, that upon arrival I just knew that I had not booked enough time in. It was too bad, I could already tell, but it always creates the drive to want to go back. With a travel bug deeply entrenched in me, it isn't too hard to twist my arm to go anywhere, but with a growing list of places I need to return to, it's all about timing and opportunity. No worries, I suppose. I'll just have to return again when the next opportunity arises.

**

Wandering through Vienna, it's easy to see the beauty of everything the Hapsburgs brought to the city. There are grand museums and palaces throughout and the centre of the city is filled with nice High Street shops and pedestrian-friendly streets.

**

Following the tips of the amazing hostess at my hostel (the fantastic Believe-It-Or-Not), I decide to go check out the Hundertwasserhaus. Friedrichshain Hundertwasser was an eccentric painter who didn't believe in straight lines. In fact, he said, "The only uncreative line is a straight one". He had a philosophy about human beings having three skins. The first was our physical skin.

The second was our clothing. The third was the buildings that we occupied.

Because of this connection to ourselves, he felt that homes needed to be integrated with our environment for us to be at harmony. He began to experiment with architecture (remember he was a painter) and the first result was the Hundertwasserhaus in Vienna. It contains no straight lines or 90-degree angles (because how can we call that a "right" angle?). Trees grow within the building and there are gardens throughout. The floors are rolling, rather than flat, mimicking the earth.

Other interesting notions that he came up with include the "right to windows". The idea with this being that an occupant in the building has the right to alter anything outside their windows within arms reach. They are free to paint it any colour or hang flowers, or whatever else they want.

The building can't be visited as people actually live there, but there is a nice little café/shop at the bottom where you can go in and have a coffee, watch a video about Hundertwasser (roughly fifteen minutes long, alternating in turn from German and English) and possibly buy any souvenirs that you might like. It was definitely worth the walk to get to. Plus, I got to indulge in my Viennese delights.

**

It's well documented that I like to try whatever the local thing is, wherever I go, so of course I had to in Vienna.

On the beverage side of things, Vienna is legendary for its cafes. Coffee culture in Vienna is still alive and well.

The local variety of coffee is the Wiener Melange, similar to a cappuccino. It's usually accompanied with a biscuit and a small glass of water (pleasant surprises to a traveller).

And, the local snack, which is always of great interest, is the Wiener Wurstel. Similar to Frankfurters, the Wieners are basically simple, skinny sausages, accompanied with a bread roll and some mustard. There is nothing too elaborate or elegant about them, and the breaking up of a hard bread roll with your own hands to stuff the Wieners in is definitely something that makes commoners of us all. I definitely made crumbs each time I tried. I challenge the business tycoons to give it a go and not seem normal.

**

With a beautiful day outside and no strong desire to spend the afternoon inside a museum, I decided to walk along the Danube Canal. There were little beach bars, similar to what I had seen along the Spree in Berlin and lots of happy people. There were stretches of grass where the exhibitionists and voyeurs alike gathered. There were even street artists, hard at work in the 30-degree heat.

**

I headed back to the Volksgarten (literally, the People's garden) and took up the opportunity to soak up some sun's rays and indulge in a book. Yes, this really was the life. Maybe they were up to something with those rankings?

Excerpt from

"Bratislava: It used to be called Pressburg. I did not know that."
(Blog post, June 18, 2011)

Well, I've been stationed in Budapest for three weeks now and I still hadn't written anything about my two-day stop in Bratislava and I was beginning to feel a bit guilty about it. I mean, I gave Hamburg an extra long account of my time there and it isn't half the city that Bratislava is (in so far as elderly prostitutes didn't once proposition me in Bratislava. Not once.). I guess it just had to do with a confluence of factors in that Bratislava (or "Brats" for fun) had the unfortunate luck of being the next stop on my trip after staying in Vienna and was a bit of a letdown and that I was eager to get going to Budapest.

In any case, the Slovakian capital managed to be a nice rest along the way and with a bit more time could be a pretty decent place to visit. I also know that it happens to have a bit of a nightlife reputation for those of you who might enjoy alkie-pops and house music. One of my new friends I made there mentioned going to a club that was under the castle hill. Subterranean dance club interest you? Then Bratislava has got you covered.

I didn't really have much of an agenda with Bratislava (becoming a theme of mine this trip) and decided to just wander around and get a feel for the place. With a compact city centre, I was able to do a bit of walking around, check out the buildings and make my way to the top where the castle resides. In my typical fashion, I like to find the highest points in any city and have a good look around. I don't know what it is, but it gives me a different perspective than street level. Oh wait, I totally know what it is: it's that I can see everything.

At the top of the Castle Hill, there is obviously a castle (which is more appropriately apparently a "fort", rather than anything regal) and great vantage points for looking around and taking pictures of everything from the Old Town to across the river at the affectionately nicknamed UFO Bridge and the Soviet-architecture side ("Do you like cold, modern, boxy buildings? Check us out!").

In the Old Town, there are all the different things one begins to expect in European cities, with interesting buildings and little town squares, and of course, delightful cafes to sip well-made (and overpriced) coffee.

In my visit I also came across things I didn't expect, such as walking into the middle of a regional conference. The Carpathian Convention (or COP3) was in town and cultural displays of the Carpathian mountains were featured on a stage for everyone to enjoy. I was able to see some traditional dancing and music from places like Poland and the Ukraine. Neat stuff, and it really impressed the Japanese tourists (is there anywhere on this planet one can travel and not run into a group of 20 Japanese tourists each clutching an SLR camera?).

I also took a walking tour that guided us around the Old Town and parts of the New Town, including standing outside the impressive Presidential Palace and the beautiful Blue Church.

As with other tours I've taken, this was a great way to get a bit of context and history on a place that I otherwise really hadn't heard too much about throughout my upbringing ("Hey, world history, next time give me a heads-up on Pressburg!").

Budapest, Or,
The Sleepy City On The Danube

"Hope"
(June 3, 2011)

I guess it's funny to start anything by thinking about something way off in the future. It doesn't make sense for some. It seems strange to be fixated on it, even. But I suppose the great human endeavour is always meant to be aiming towards a destination. We all just want to get somewhere. It becomes cliché that the journey is actually more important than the destination, and I suppose that is true in some respects. We experience a great many things along the way and grow as human beings. I won't deny that. But, perhaps, if I can be so bold, I think the catalyst for all those journeys comes from having a destination in the first place. Things rarely come to us in a ray of light and revelation as we sit on our sofas eating potato chips and watching movies stretched over commercial breaks on cable television. No to have even the bare minimum amount of experience in the world, stepping out into it is necessary. There are people who quit, though. Those people are the ones who don't have any hope. They ask what is the point, and they mean it. They have lost all purpose and drive. There is no light at the end of the tunnel. There is only a dark tunnel that they have chosen to lie down in and die. That is the truth. It is hard and it hurts. It can reach deep inside someone and tear them apart like a swallowed razor. A brutal example, to be sure, but necessary to describe how awful that existence can be. It really is up to us. We can choose to dwell on the tunnels that we get caught in or we can create lights that guide us and pull us forward through life. We can get dragged through amazing experiences, but we have to open ourselves up to the possibility. Without hope, that light, well, what good can we be? We can stand still and let the world spin around us in clockwork, counting down our days until we finally vacate this planet. It's a horrible thought, but that's the way it can be. No, it's better still to push forward, in search of whatever it is that we are in search of. There are a great number of people who are truly unhappy. That is a fact that is certainly indisputable. They want to push forward, to find that missing whatever, but they give up. They lack hope. They lack the idea of possibility. It doesn't even have to be probable, just possible. Hope is not a guarantee. It is the very slimmest of chances that flickers way off in the distance. It sounds unimpressive, but like the smallest drop of water to a man dying in the desert it can mean the greatest of difference. Hope comes in many forms. Indeed, I actually believe that each person carries within themselves their own idea of hope. It comes in the shape and size and tastes of whomever it belongs. It won't be the exact same thing that drives every man and woman to keep pushing on with life. No, of course not, we are all different. However, we are all very much the same. We are complex, though delicate, creatures who are built with the capacity to achieve great things when we throw our everything in. The thing that can actually pull us all in, that warm glow that calls out to our freezing selves, is hope. Our own hopes, designed to each of us.

**

Nan sat at the end of the couch, tucked under her Afghan blanket. She had nodded off and was beginning to snore. Lois looked at her and smiled at the small trickle of drool that was working its way down Nan's chin. They had eaten garlic linguini for dinner and pasta always made her grandmother tired. Nan had insisted, despite Lois' suggestions, that they have pasta that night. It was Tuesday and Tuesday was pasta night. Last week it had been fettuccini with an alfredo sauce. The week before it had been stuffed ravioli with a tomato and cheese sauce. Lois was glad that Nan was at least flexible enough to allow different pastas. It wasn't that her grandmother was stubborn, although she could be; it was mostly that her grandmother was very superstitious. She had yelled at Lois when they were out for a walk once for stepping on cracked pavement. Nan felt that it was tremendous bad luck. Lois thought that it was a negligent city council. There was really no way to tell,

as far as Lois was concerned. Everything happened.
It was unclear whether everything happened for a
reason, or even if some things happened for reasons.
The only certainty was that things happened. Even then,
Lois was carrying her doubts. She had seen strange and
absurd things occur in her twenty-seven years on this
spinning orb that made her seriously doubt if they did
happen. You know those moments when time just
seems to stop and you want to turn to anyone,
a stranger even, and ask "Did that just happen?"
Lois had those all the time. There was now a large blur
for her between what really did happen and what she
thought may or may not have happened. She didn't think
that she suffered from any mental illness, and as far as
any actual medical practitioners were concerned,
Lois was perfectly sane. But there are doubts that linger
and remain nonetheless. It was all part of the human
experience, she thought. It was the same way that
people could speak of divine acts or other worlds.
She didn't think that she had actually witnessed ghosts
or angels or aliens or anything like that. No, Lois felt that
she had just seen the wacky milieu of humanity
throughout her life. What did it all mean? Why were we
here? Hard questions to answer, to be sure.

Since she had lost her mother everything seemed to
change for Lois. It wasn't that her mother had died;
it was more that she just got lost. It was much the same
way that socks sometimes enter the dryer in a pair and
leave alone. Lois had grown distant and done the routine
daughter things and called and visited, but it didn't seem
to click. In what seemed to come out of the blue she
arrived one afternoon at her mother's home to find a very
different woman living there. Literally, it was another
person. She was taller and younger than Lois' mum and
had a different name. She was actually a very pleasant
woman, someone that Lois wouldn't mind socialising
with without any familial ties, but that is not what had
dragged her there. Inquiring about the woman that lived
there that was actually related to Lois, there was very
little information to be had. Yes, she had moved.
No, she didn't leave an address. Sorry, I can't make tea

on Saturday. Lois was at an end. The woman who had presumably given birth to her and raised her into the woman that she was had disappeared.

Disappearances are generally a pretty awful thing, though in the case of Lois' mother it turned out to be more of an occurrence, something to mention like the weather and the football score. The main thing that affected Lois in losing her mum, other than saving on the transit fare to the other side of town to visit, was the dawning on her that she was now the person solely responsible for caring for Nan. Lois' grandmother, whom we know as Nan, the woman asleep on the sofa, drooling, was the mother of Lois' father. Lois had lost her father when she was eight. They had been playing hide and seek, which made the situation very strange indeed. There were rumours that swirled through their neighbourhood that Thom Atkins had been swept away by the current of the river that passed behind their home. Lois chose to believe that her father was actually a very good hider and was still waiting for her to find him. The first couple of days she spent tirelessly searching behind the cupboard and underneath the bathroom sink. Eventually she had to return to school, but every morning and when Lois returned home in the late afternoon, she would spend her free time seeking her daddy. It was at that time that her Nan came to live with Lois and her mother. The woman cared for Lois and doted on her in the way that grandmothers do dote.

Nearly twenty years later, it was Lois caring for Nan. The funniest part, Lois would swear later, was that she never remembered Nan moving in with her. Lois had moved out of her mother's home at twenty and lived a very independent lifestyle, only popping back to her then-not-missing mum's house for scheduled tea or dinners. Nan, the mother-in-law to Lois' mother, had stayed with her missing husband's then-not-missing wife. Over the years, though, Lois had always made a point of having her grandmother visit for dinners and because of the late hours that they would spend chatting, she would insist upon her Nan staying over.

There was always a bed for Nan at Lois' apartment. That was made clear. Time moved on and the frequency of their dinners increased. So much so, that Lois barely noticed that her Nan had virtually moved in. Sure, most of her possessions remained at Lois' mother's home, but the spare bedroom in Lois' apartment was beginning to get that old woman look. There was a lot of talcum powder. Lois was unclear on what talcum powder was. She had her doubts that Nan knew, but she didn't want to ask, for fear that the stubborn old woman would force more superstition on her. Monday might be talc day, for goodness sake. It might just be one of those things that you do, even if no one can explain it. So, needless to say, when Lois' mum disappeared, she realised that she was now the sole person to care for Nan. She did wonder what happened to all of her Nan's stuff that was left at her mum's place, but after a further examination of the "guest" bedroom, found it chock-a-block with old lady curios and collectibles. There were small porcelain dolls and mahogany jewellery chests galore. Lois really had no idea where and when they came from. She certainly didn't notice that a wrought-iron four-poster had replaced the generic bed frame she had purchased from a large Scandinavian furniture chain. When did that come in, she asked herself. Lois couldn't remember moving any furniture, actually. Her living room had one of those pneumatic armchairs that lifted up and down and left to right and vibrated like a cheap ride outside the supermarket. Lois definitely did not remember when that arrived. It just seemed like it had always been there. Had it? No, of course it hadn't. There was a time that this apartment was a proper flat for a young woman. There were no pneumatic armchairs and there was no talc! But when? Lois could not say. Everything happened, was all she could try and comfort herself with. It became far too upsetting to try and consider if there was a rhyme or reason to it. Lois Atkins was a twenty-seven year old bookstore clerk who lived with her eighty-three year old Nan. That was certain, probably. Everything outside of that, in the city and the world at large was hearsay. She had heard of all sorts of exciting things, but until she could touch, taste, or smell them, they really did not exist. The internet just seemed like a magic box filled with random, disparate ideas. Who could make sense of it all? What purpose did it serve? How was it even a web? That was too much for her. Lois wanted to know. She really did. However, at this point in time, all she was certain of was that Tuesday was pasta night. Even that was due to the decree of her lodger/grandmother.

Yes, to Lois, Nan was a woman who had it all figured out. There was no messing about with Nan. Nan had lived in part of nine decades, which is remarkable in some ways, and absolutely prosaic in others. Well, of course she had, thought Lois, she's in her eighties. That is how mathematics works. On the subject of math, Lois wondered if there was some magic formula that her grandmother had held onto for all these years.
It was why she humoured the old woman's superstitions. What if there was some logic to it? Lois didn't actually believe in any of them. No, she felt she was too rational for that. Although, she carried many doubts about her own rationality, too. It was more that she didn't want to offend the old woman, and she didn't mind, if indeed the superstitions were true, if some good luck rubbed off in her own direction. It wasn't an entirely selfish thought. Lois just felt that, if good and bad luck existed, it was better to try and play a bit by the rules. Due to her own disbelief, Lois was actually quite horrible at following the rules on her own. She walked under ladders, crossed the paths of black cats, spilled table salt, and had broken a couple mirrors. To be fair, she had justified to herself, that pocket mirror was very flimsy and had been banged around pretty good at the bottom of her purse.
In the presence of Nan, however, Lois followed every superstitious instruction. If life really was a cosmic battle between the forces of good and bad chance, Lois hoped to break even. The hardest thing about following Nan's superstitious behaviour was the overall illogic to it. Lois couldn't see the A to B in it. How exactly would breaking a mirror bring seven years of bad luck? Nan was a kindly old woman, if a bit stern, and had managed to survive all

these years living by an unexplainable code. Lois had heard her say many times that everything happened for a reason. Lois just wanted an explanation. Why, exactly, did that happen? That was it. In a stupidly serene way the old woman would just shrug it off and say that axiom of wisdom again. Lois really had no answer to the non-answer. The only thing she was certain of was that everything happened, and even then, she carried her doubts.

The weather forecast was just finishing and Lois was depressed by the predictions for rain and thundershowers. The weathergirl sent the broadcast back to the anchor desk. The dull gray anchor smiled dumbly at the camera and instructed the viewers not to go away during the commercial break; the lottery was coming up next. Lois got up and went to the kitchen to make herself a cup of tea. She found the electric kettle and filled it just past the minimum notch in the side. The coil inside always frightened her that it might burn the entire apartment down. She had once filled the water up just below the minimum level and only really noticed after she had flicked the switch to start the boiling. For whatever reason (if things truly do happen for a reason), Lois left it, but watched with great intent. She nervously monitored the kettle, hoping that her flat wouldn't go down in a quick ball of fire all because she wanted a cup of Sleepytime. Luckily (if luck truly does exist), no fire occurred. Lois was able to have her tea, which actually came as a great relief to the newfound stress that had enveloped her. Ever since, she had made darn sure to fill at least slightly above the minimum notch. While she waited for the water to boil, Lois rummaged through the cupboard trying to decide what type of tea to have. One of the benefits of living with an elderly woman was an abundance of tea. Lois found a strong Rooisbos that she quite liked. It was just past dinner, so she felt it was early enough to still have a caffeinated tea. It didn't really matter, too much, as Lois always found it quite easy to get to sleep. Yes, she thought, a nice soothing Rooibos tea. She might even have a bubble bath with aromatic candles. That would be very relaxing, indeed. It was in this moment of pre-serenity that a loud shriek came from the living room.

Lois ran into the room to check on Nan and saw the old woman covered in tears running down her face, meeting the spittle at her chin. There was something quite odd about her.

"Nan, what's wrong?"

"I've won."

"What?"

"I've won the lottery."

"What?"

"They just read out my numbers, all six of them."

"Really?"

"Yes. I'm shocked."

"I didn't even know you bought a ticket this week."

"I buy a ticket every week, my dear."

"You do?"

"Yes, of course. You can't win unless you do."

"I don't understand."

"About thirty years ago I bought a lottery ticket. They gave me six random numbers. I had a good feeling about them and that week I won a free ticket. I asked for the same numbers the next week. I've been getting the same numbers every week since. I didn't even win another free ticket after that first time. But, I thought those were my numbers and you can't change now. You just can't. So I have been waiting and I just knew that eventually my time would come."

"You know the odds are astronomically impossible to win, right?"

"But I just did, Lois. I just won. They read my numbers out."

"That's amazing, Nan. I don't know what to say. What do we do? Is there a number we call or do we go down to the head office for the lottery? I'm just so stunned."

"You know I'll give you a little spending money, my dear."

"Sure, you don't have to, Nan, really, but thank you."

"Oh, it's the least I could do."

"Do you mind me seeing the ticket? I don't really care about the money, I just want to see and hold the lucky ticket."

"Sure, let me go grab it from my purse. I always carry my ticket in my purse."

Nan got up from the sofa and left the living room.
Lois' head was spinning. This was insane. This was one of those moments where she wanted to scream from the rooftops "Did this just happen?" but she actually felt like she was losing her voice. This was incredible and overwhelming. Imagine, she thought, her Nan spending thirty years playing the same numbers and eventually winning the jackpot at eighty-three years old.
They will make a movie about her. She'll be a celebrity!
Nan, her Nan, will be famous. Where was Nan?
What was keeping her?

Lois walked into Nan's room to see her sitting on the side of the bed, with her purse on her lap. Lois sat down next to her and put her arm around her.

"Are you alright, Nan?"

"It's not here."

"Did you leave it somewhere else?"

"No."

"What about in the kitchen drawer with your receipts?"

"No, it won't be there."

"Where is it?"

"I don't know. I didn't buy it this week."

"What?"

"Yesterday, Monday, is my normal day when I buy my lottery ticket for the Tuesday night draw. I didn't buy it yesterday."

"No?"

"No, I had meant to. I had gone out for the groceries and I brought back almost everything I had meant to."

"Did you pick up yoghurt?"

"No, Lois, I forgot that too."

"I'm so sorry Nan."

"It is just yoghurt, Lois."

"I meant the jackpot."

"It's okay, everything happens for a reason."

Lois looked at the frail old body of her grandmother and wanted to hold her in her arms forever.

"Are you sure you're okay?"

"Yes, I'm fine."

"Really?"

"Yes, I'll just leave a note on the fridge to make sure I buy my ticket next week."

"Regrets"
(June 6, 2011)

Fuck. That's an awful word to use, but one that appears
more often than not when contemplating the impact of
our previous actions. We tread heavily on this earth,
physically and metaphorically, and leave the imprints of
stomped boots everywhere. It's far stronger than simply
leaving footprints in the sand. Those are quite beautiful
and we know, because of everything that science and
experience tells us, that they are not permanent.
They can be plodded over or washed away. It doesn't
matter how, all we know is that they will not be there
forever. Real life isn't like that. We go storming ahead,
often unaware of everyone that we will encounter.
We will run into people. That is a fact. We will even run
over people. That is also a fact. It's in our nature, simple
beasts that we are, to go running at all. With our eyes
way out ahead, looking for whatever it is that drives us,
we'll forget all those that we trample underfoot.
Well, sometimes, at least, we will. No, it is far more likely
that long after we've left them to eat the dust of our
wake, we'll stop and realise that they even existed.
That's when we begin to feel awful. It's a horrible sinking
feeling inside. You know what it is. You've felt it.
You regret doing it. Yes, yes, those awful regrets.
Why do they fester inside us like that? They aren't very
good at much, are they? No, they can't help us time
travel. There is no benefit to them in that regard.
We can't unring a bell or unbreak a glass orb.
We're stuck living in the results and not the actions.
Oh, those wretched actions! They should not have
happened, we will tell ourselves. How could I do that?
How? Am I a monster? I feel so bad. I feel so bad, you
know that I do. I feel. They, the victims, they feel, too.
That's what causes those regrets. It's the knowledge that
something we've done or didn't do did or didn't happen.
It's the knowledge that at a specific point in time it was
supposed to not happen or happen and it did or didn't.

It's the haunting knowledge that now, in the present, and worse still, in the vast future, no action can change that moment in the past. That is regret! People throw slogans around that they live for no regrets. Oh, what a pleasant world that would be. They miss the meaning. They actually just get half of it, but with a dumb ignorance to it all. They use the slogan that when presented with an opportunity, the answer will always be yes. They will always do that thing. That thing will always happen. When confronted, they will say, quite simply, "no regrets". So callous! The odds tell us that at best, they'll be right half the time. They'll please those who were meant to be pleased some of the time. Unfortunately, they will also hurt those who could be hurt some of the time. It's hardly better than the person with no system at all. It might even be worse, because they've created a moral code of their own, the one of not missing any experience. They are hedonists of the highest order! That might be fine, if we were all hedonists. But we are not. Along their paths they'll meet someone who holds some things sacred. They will take that person's cherished chalices and smash them against the ground if an opportunity appears. Yes, they live for tomorrow. Regrets are for yesterday. But time is not linear, despite all rational attempts to control it. Even in the moments of today, the mind can drift away to thoughts of the possible future and the regrettable past. They are no less real to you than the physical things that assure you of today. They are a part of you, each. Regret can be an awful thing to carry with you forward, but it is there. There is no denying that.

Excerpt from
"Delicate Arms"
(Unpublished novel)

Harvey Hudson was a completely despicable looking man. He was morbidly obese and his face seemed to be scowling as a default. Surely it would become even more menacing if he were truly upset, Ralph reasoned.
Of course, being an ideologue at ends with the Enlightenment and everything wonderful that had spun off from it, Hudson was always upset. Unlike many good-natured conservatives who hoped to revive bygone days, Harvey Hudson was a man who wanted to bring back the Middle Ages. He had no tolerance for opposing views and got irritated at the very mention of anything that even slightly sounded progressive. How Ralph Kirk found himself sitting at the same luncheon table with him was unknown, but the thought of it made him extremely nervous. Ralph was not a liberal ideologue and was open to accepting other worldviews if they were put forth in cogent argument. However, he was very much a fan of possessing rights, accepting responsibilities, and believed, naively perhaps, that humanity had improved since the 1200s.

"Do you know what we're having for lunch, pal?"

Ralph looked to his sides to see whom Hudson was addressing. As both seats were vacant, it appeared that it was he.

"Um, no, I don't know for sure. I had heard something about roast duck."

"Hmm, good. I like roast duck. As long as they don't mess around with any of that Paki shit. I don't want a curry sauce on my duck. I just want it cooked the way my Grandma would roast a duck, you know?"

"Uh, right. I've only had duck once before. I don't know how they cooked it."

"Where did you have it?"

"It was at a restaurant."

A Chinese restaurant.

"You probably had that French shit. Duck a la orange, right?"

The way Hudson pronounced "orange" in American English seemed put-on.

"Yeah, maybe. I don't know much about food."

Hudson laughed.

"You can tell that I do, though, right?"

Ralph laughed nervously.

"Let me tell you, pal, I've been going to conferences and conventions like this for thirty years and it becomes a goddamned pleasure when they don't serve one of two things."

"Which two?"

"Well, the standard for a luncheon at one of these midrange business hotels is a basic chicken breast, some potatoes and mixed vegetables. I like that usually, but you get sick of it eventually. The other thing they sometimes serve is whatever the latest ethnic craze is. I don't want quinoa or lentils for lunch. Spare me, am I right?"

Were lentils really ethnic? Ralph wasn't sure. He thought they were pretty basic staples. Hudson probably thought that rice was off limits, too.

"Yeah, right."

"What's your name, pal?"

"Ralph, Mr. Hudson, my name is Ralph Kirk."

"Please, call me Harvey. Only my prostitute and my doctor are allowed to call me Mr. Hudson."

Was he joking? Did he go to prostitutes? That would be a huge scandal. He must be joking. Of course, Ralph had heard about that painkiller scandal from a few years back. Anything was possible.

"Ah, I see."

"I'm joking, Ralph!"

Ralph laughed nervously while Harvey Hudson let out a large belly laugh.

"Yes, yes, of course I let my doctor call me Harvey."

"Of course."

"So, Ralph, what brings you here? You from stateside? You look like a New Englander. I'm hoping more Connecticut than Vermont, if you catch my drift."

"Oh, no, Harvey. I'm Canadian."

Harvey's normal scowl turned into a more definite frown.

"A Canadian? Hmm, aren't you fellas all commies?"

"No, not really. We have a Conservative government, too."

"Please, Ralph. Don't tell me about what is and isn't conservative. I wrote the goddamned book. Seven of them, actually. All of them best sellers. You guys up there are all commies."

"No, I'm fairly certain I still have private property."

Hudson looked Ralph sternly in the eyes.

"What do you do, Ralph?"

"I was a banker, actually, and am in a bit of a transition phase, career wise."

"A transition phase? Sounds like you are unemployed."

"From The End of Time"
(June 15, 2011)

Then, as if to call a cosmic bluff, it was over.

**

A white man in a lab coat spoke to the reporter and said that this was the greatest computer that had ever been built before. In front of them stood a miniscule plastic rectangle, no bigger than a credit card.

"It's a supercomputer!"

"Yeah, that's cool. Just give me a second, I'm making dinner reservations."

"But you aren't speaking on the phone."

"Yeah, I know, I'm just booking it online."

"You can do that?"

"Yeah, it's a smart phone. You don't have one?"

"No."

"You're the head scientist on a so-called supercomputer and you don't have a smart phone?"

"No."

"You should get one."

"What can they do?"

"Oh, just about anything, man. You can go on the internet, listen to music, watch videos, take pictures, read a book."

"Wow, that's incredible!"

"What does your supercomputer do again?"

"It's pretty good at chess."

"Oh."

"Do you want to take a picture?"

"I already did. Listen, this is boring me. I'm going to go catch the bus that is going to be at the stop two blocks away in six minutes. Later."

**

A white man in a lab coat spoke to the reporters and said that this was the greatest computer that had ever been built before. In front of them stood a large, metal machine the size of a pick-up truck.

"What can it do?"

"It's a supercomputer, it can do just about anything."

"Can it solve complex abstract brain puzzlers?"

"No, it can't do that."

"Can it create poetry?"

"No, it can't do that."

"Can it come up with the funniest joke known to mankind?"

"No, it can't do any of that stuff!"

"Well, what can it do?"

"It can do math, really, really fast."

"How fast?"

"Faster than you or me and faster than the old supercomputer."

"Oh."

"You aren't impressed?"

"I was hoping for something more."

"It's smaller than the old computer."

"That's something, I guess."

A polite applause occurred. No photographers were present, but a small blurb appeared on the seventh page of the paper.

**

A white man in a lab coat spoke to the reporters and said that this was the greatest computer that had ever been built before. In front of them stood a large, metal machine the size of a gymnasium.

"What can it do?"

"It's a supercomputer, what can't it do, lads?"

"But, specifically, what can it do?"

"You know your son's fourth grade mathematics homework?"

"Yes."

"How long does it take him to do every night?"

"An hour."

"This supercomputer can do those same calculations – in half the time."

The reporters applauded and flash bulbs went off.

**

The crowd gasped with astonishment as they looked
upon the latest work from the polymath genius.
A rapturous applause followed and a bow from the
maestro himself. The head of the merchant's guild,
the very man who had commissioned this work
announced that the painter/sculptor/inventor/scientist
would be joining him for dinner, and that they must be
getting along. They started walking down the road
towards the merchant's manor. A throng of people
followed, as not a person short of a throng would be
enough to describe how popular the genius was.

One man stood back and stared at the work. He looked
with intent, and then for kicks, he tried looking without
intent. He looked it up and down. He looked it right and
left. He held one eye open and the other shut. He did the
opposite. Finally, after a long sigh, he announced that he
"just didn't get it."

**

Emilio sat in a tavern, drinking putrid wine mixed with
choleric water ("for taste"). He had done the same every
night for the last ten years of his life. Before that, he had
preferred to sleep right after his supper. Much of that
decision had been because of the physical
attractiveness of his wife. Ten years and eleven children
later had taken most of the beauty away from Emilio's
wife. What beauty was left appeared between the hours
that Emilio returned home from the tavern and the dawn.
This time was also known as "night" or "you know, that
time when things are absolutely pitch black and it is
really hard to see exactly what is going on." It was then
that Emilio could touch and caress his wife. Part of that
was the absolute darkness and the other part was
Emilio's absolute drunkenness. That's how, despite his
reluctance to otherwise touch his wife, Emilio had
regularly fornicated with her and produced eleven
children, seven of which happened past the point that
Emilio, or most men, would describe her as "doable."

On this particular night at the tavern, Emilio had been thinking about nothing related to his wife, which was a change. Indeed the tavern owner had noticed that Emilio's normal demeanour, a rather dark and glum way of living, was completely lifted. Wondering what it was that had made Emilio so glad, the owner went over and asked him. Emilio smiled, leaned in forward and whispered a blasphemous thought. The tavern owner frowned at first and walked away, without saying anything. The thought trickled through his brain and he began to consider the possibility.

After Emilio had left, a third man, a rather bright fellow who had been working for the local land baron asked the tavern owner what it was that Emilio had told him. The tavern owner, now with a smile, leaned in forward and whispered that blasphemous thought. The third man frowned for barely a second and then smiled himself.

**

Pablo the Assistant to the Inquisitor walked with some trepidation into the chamber of the Grand Inquisitor. He knew that the Big Guy was in a foul mood and had not wanted to be disturbed by anyone. Unfortunately, with the latest news that had arrived at the front door just minutes ago, Pablo felt like he had no choice. He breathed in heavily and stepped forward. Hearing a presence, the Grand Inquisitor appropriately inquired as to why he was being bothered.

"Who comes here?"

"It's I, Pablo, your Inquisitiveness."

"Why are you here, Pablo?"

"Well, it's just that I bring news, your Questionable One."

"What is the news?"

"We've just received word that there are a bunch of heretics in the town, your Inquisitiveness."

"Why must they always be heretics?"

"Indeed, sir, I agree. It's an awful business, that. I would have preferred something a bit more interesting. Witches would be fun, right?"

"What would be fun about that?"

"I don't really know, your Inquisitiveness, but a change is as good as a rest, I hear."

"Where did you hear that from?"

"Do you know Emilio? Juan's son? He told me."

"Where is this Emilio?"

"I don't really know, sir, it's a nice day out, he might have gone to the beach or maybe he's lying on the grass, soaking up the sun."

"Would you like to go to the beach, Pablo?"

"Yes, sir, I would, sir, if it weren't too much trouble."

"Where is my beach towel?"

**

Kyle the Reluctant Viking was not entirely convinced with the whole idea of raping and pillaging. He felt it was in conflict with the whole general community ethos that the Danes had firmly established at home. Widely regarded as a warm and loving group of chaps when sitting around eating herring and talking about all the great stuff that Odin has done, Kyle couldn't understand why they had to be such great big dicks when they vacationed. The whole concept seemed quite strange to him.

"I am not one man here and another there, fellows. I just don't like being inconsistent with who I am. My wife doesn't like it either. She says that I need to be a consistent individual to be a proper role model for our children. Maybe I should look into some sort of domestic occupation. I am quite good at carpentry, perhaps I can stick around here and build and repair furniture."

The community council, filled with proper Vikings just stared at Kyle with eyes filled with the thunder and lightning of Thor.

"I mean, perhaps I could do the carpentry thing in our new colonies. I've heard lovely things about Iceland. I hear it's not that bad, actually."

Erik the Ill-Tempered, a horrible and despicable brute (and naturally, the leader of the community), stood up, ready to give the verdict about Kyle's future. His long hair was bleached blonde from the sun. His beard had flecks of food stuck in it that no one, not even his wife, was willing to tell him about. He was a man's man and a Viking's Viking.

"Kyle, I give you my blessing. It will be tough to see you go, but if it is making you unhappy, you shouldn't do it. We all just want you to be happy."

Kyle was astonished. That was not the judgment he was expecting at all.

"Really? Erik, that's fantastic. I didn't expect you all to be so understanding."

"Of course we are understanding. We are all family. We only want what's best for everyone."

"What about the raping and pillaging?"

"Well, there's that, too. It's not to everyone's taste."

"You're not so ill-tempered after all, Erik."

"No, I don't know where that name came from. It might possibly be wordplay because my father was known as Erik the Irritable. It's not spot-on like your name, Kyle the Reluctant. That's you to a T, isn't it?"

"Yes. I suppose it is quite accurate. I'd prefer something a bit more positive. Reluctance seems to be frowned upon. Perhaps I could be called Kyle the Peaceful, or Kyle the Cautious."

"Is it alright if we don't change your name? It would just be really confusing to all of us, and we'd have to keep track of it. Leif has already changed his name seven times. It made us all so upset that we gave him his eighth and final name, Leif the Asshole."

**

In the middle of a wild wine-filled orgy, one Roman cried out to no one in particular, asking, "Is this all life is meant to be?" Without delay every soul, all one hundred and thirty-three there, including the seven senators, called back, "Yes!"

**

The hot red stuff really caught everyone by surprise. Because it was bright and new, naturally they all wanted to get their hands on it. Archibald Hieronymus Humboldt Oglington the Fifth, or "Og" as he was called, tried to warn his friends. Unfortunately, due to a limited vocabulary, his explanation was quite vague and slightly confusing. Trying to explain that fire was bad caused the group to rush to destroy it, while explaining that fire was also good left them scratching their heads, before trying to stick their hairy hands back into the fire.

The by-product of this poor decision was that the smell of burning flesh was discovered to be actually quite pleasant to this crowd, who until now had only eaten raw meat and those mean red berries that gave them tummy aches. After a few false starts, and several multiple degree burns, some mammoth meat was thrown on the fire and the first barbeque happened. Like any good barbeque it led to painful headaches the next day and a big mess that no one felt like cleaning up.

204

**

In the beginning was the light. Some said that it was good, while others harboured doubts.

Excerpt from
"Budapest: City of Leisure"
(Blog post, June 18, 2011)

Are you an uptight workaholic who is afraid to unwind? Stay outta Budapest, pal. This city is for living life and not getting all wound up in the trivial stuff.

It took me awhile to figure this out. I have been in the city for three weeks and was having trouble describing it to people. What was the general pulse of the place? How do you define the ineffable? A lot of places I've travelled I can usually get pegged in a day or two of wandering around, observing the natural comings and goings of the city dwellers and what seems to make them tick. Budapest was a much tougher nut to crack and I was stumped to why that was. The first thing people ask is whether the city is beautiful. A reasonable question to ask as every picture of the city on the internet is loaded with beauty. In reality, yes, it is just as pretty as those pictures.

It also has a bit of grime to it. Not a bad sort of grime, but just a settled, lived-in kind. This isn't a tourist attraction like Disneyland where the park closes and people leave. This is a major city that has people of all walks of life interspersed with all the lovely tourist attractions. That's the big thing. People live here.

To further that, I have to mention that I mean they "live" in all senses of the word. They occupy space here, inhabiting buildings, etc. But they also enjoy their time doing it. It's not about a day-to-day grind. It's about just being.

The first week I was here I couldn't understand it at all. There I would be, going for a run through the park on a business day and it would be jam-packed with people of all ages and perceivable socio-economic statuses.

They'd be walking around, hand-in-hand, or sharing a beer or some wine. They'd be playing in the playgrounds, fathers and mothers with their children. They'd have pickup games of soccer and basketball in the many free facilities. They'd be lying on the ground, soaking up the sun's rays (tops optional). I'd continue on with my run in the 30-degree heat, convinced that I was the hardest working person there (and I'm on vacation).

But, that's not it at all. Hungarians aren't lazy, they just know not to sweat the small stuff and to enjoy what the day has to offer. If the weather is gorgeous, what better time to spend with the ones you love? There are free concerts all over the city and as many diversions as there are hours in the day (in just the City Park, there is a zoo, a bathhouse, a circus, an amusement park, and a bunch of museums). I've definitely embraced that mentality and that's part of the reason that my blog posts have become infrequent. You can forgive me if I'd prefer to lie in the grass and read a book under the sun, yes?

Of course, my own traits are hard to shake completely. One day I found a hill in the park that had lots of sun and decided to spread a towel out and read, soaking up the Vitamin D. My tan so far this summer is relatively faint (with the typical exception of farmer's tanned neck/arms), so I decided to get rid of a bit of the milky white on my back. I tried to lie there and relax and dive deep into Dostoevsky (nearly finished the Brothers Karamazov), but wouldn't it just happen that a swarm of Hungarian bees arrive. I tend to get annoyed by a single fly landing on me, so having fifty bees tickling my bare legs and back was not at all pleasant. I swatted them away the best that I could, but they would not relent. I looked around at the other sun worshippers on the hill and they were all unbothered. In fact, even the nearly-nudes were having no issues and they had the most skin exposed to this onslaught of us all. I had to sit there and bear the bees until I could finish my beer and pack up and leave. Needless to say I haven't quite got past Dmitri's trial.

**

If I wasn't quite able to unwind on a hill infested with bees, well then at least I could enjoy a traditional Turkish bathhouse. The first night that I arrived in Budapest I went with two friends that I had met in Bratislava to the Rudas baths for a Saturday co-ed night. Typically, at many bathhouses there are segregated bathing periods by gender during the days. When this happens, the women supposedly wear a toga-like item and the men wear loincloths. One of the other things to scare off (or entice, I guess) potential bathers is that certain baths on certain days have a reputation as being a place for gay cruising. One such description in my Lonely Planet guidebook says that on Tuesdays you can expect "intense cruising" at a particular bathhouse. Not remotely interested in that type of experience and not blessed with a command of the Hungarian language to turn away advances ("Csak hadd fürödjön!"), I definitely saw the benefits of just going on a "normal" co-ed night.

On co-ed night at Rudas, the opening hours are from 10pm to 4am, which is a really cool idea in theory, but definitely dangerously late for a group of weary Western travellers who took a 6am train from Bratislava that morning. Instead of loincloths or togas, normal swimwear is required. "Normal" being a relative term, as anything from banana slings to long trunks were worn by the men (note to any male considering a skimpy bathing suit, after consulting with my female friends, you basically have to be built like Daniel Craig to pull it off, so don't humiliate yourself, mate). Each bather is given a wristband with an RFID tag in it that unlocks your own personal cabana changing room, where you can safely store all your belongings. It was a pretty cool experience to know that you have your own personal locker that you can climb into.

After changing, you make your way through the showers and give yourself a rinse before you enter the baths. In the centre of the bathhouse was a large warm bath underneath a dome that had small coloured circular skylights. There were four additional baths (one in each corner of the room), each with a different temperature, ranging from coldish-lukewarm all the way to toasty. There were a couple side rooms as well, one with a very chilly bath, another with a steam room, and a wing that had three different sauna rooms (each of intensifying temperature).

What to say about spending about four hours in varying temperatures of water? It was damned relaxing and a very enjoyable experience. The fact that I woke up the next day with the sniffles was totally worth it (and to be fair, I had felt a cold coming on a day or two earlier). If you have the chance, I do think that a midnight trip to a bathhouse is a requisite activity for a visit to Budapest.

Excerpt from

"Budapest: Another Day at the Zoo"
(Blog post, June 19, 2011)

On another sticky hot afternoon in Pest I decided to head to see the local Budapest Zoo and Botanical Gardens, hoping that it would be a nice way to spend the day. I could not have been more pleased as this gem, located on the north end of the City Park is possibly the nicest zoo that I've ever been to. It wasn't the largest zoo, but going at a reasonable pace you can see pretty much everything in two and a half hours, so it is well worth a visit, and for the equivalent of ten bucks, not an expensive afternoon.

Back to the beauty part! Unlike some zoos that go out of their way to remind you that you're basically visiting an animal prison, complete with concrete walls and iron bars, the Budapest Zoo prides itself on its appearances. Yes, it still keeps animals in captivity under display (we can get into the pros and cons of this another time), but it gives them a nice habitat. There are lots of charming buildings that resemble a medieval village and then the foliage throughout the park lives up to the botanical gardens part of the name (don't ask me to name plants, I'm not a botanist).

Excerpt from

"Delicate Arms"

(Unpublished novel)

Vacations can be a bit of a drag, in the end. There are
obviously lots of great things about travelling, but there
are always downsides, too. The excitement of being able
to go is usually met with the frustration of actually going.
There are flights involved, and flights mean that there
will be security and customs and checked luggage.
It's a big hassle and inevitably if you travel enough times
you will have issues. You might get stuck in security
being patted down by everyone's version of a nightmare
groper. You might be interrogated at customs about the
value of a pair of athletic socks you bought one day at
a sports store in Newcastle. You'll say that you paid
ninety-nine pence, because they were on sale in
a discount bin. Customs will claim that they were worth
seven pounds because they feature the logo of
an internationally recognised brand name (despite that
brand name being known for using cheap labour in third
world countries). You'll wonder why this is an issue at all,
even if they did cost seven pounds. They are hardly in
the same category of danger to the Canadian
countryside as boots covered in mud from
a BSE-contaminated farm (the last time you take the
advice of a Welshman for a "neat" place to check out).
They won't be undercutting the revenue of an alternative
domestic retailer, unlike those bottles of whisky that you
most certainly won't be declaring (the only declaration is
that bottles of 18 year old Glenlivet, 16 year old
Distiller's Edition Lagavulin, and Isle of Jura Superstition
purchased in a Scotland supermarket for the same price
as purchasing just the Lagavulin in Canada is a crime).
But, of course, that can only be declared if your luggage
(which may or may not contain whisky) actually arrives
safely. It is a guarantee in life, that if you travel enough
times, you will have bags go missing.

Sometimes it is explained in the most routine manner of ways by the authorities.

"We didn't load them on the plane."

Well, of course, that would be the most logical thing to do. Why would any of us want our bags on a trip, the damned things just weigh so much and would really be a drag if we had to carry them every where. You've done us a great favour, mate. I appreciate that. Now, what to do about a change of clothes? These socks have to go. Oh, you know of a shopping mall nearby? Perfect. I'll see if I can get any on sale.

"Is there an address we can reach you at?"

Yes, it's my home address. The place I just left. Have the bags sent back there. I'll pick them up when I return in a few weeks.

"We can give you a call when they turn up."

Excellent. I'll just leave my phone on then, with international roaming fees, just to wait for you to call. Fantastic idea. Let's do this. Also, I suppose I can't be out exploring and touring the city because the window that you'd want to return the bags in would be really small. Oh, it's actually a large window? Even better. I will sit in my room and wait between eleven and six for the bags to arrive. Best possible use of my time in such a short visit to a world-class city. It's all right; I suppose I can make up for it by scheduling a flight back during an airline strike. That will give me plenty of time.

"I Am The Dust"
(June 22, 2011)

It was getting late and I had grown tired of Celeste's
company. It wasn't that she wasn't a pretty or bright
thing, but I guess I just didn't see the same glow from
her that others did.

"Would you be offended if I said I was getting tired,
Celeste?"

She looked at me with those sweet, pretty green eyes.

"No, I don't suppose I would be offended. Are you going
straight to bed?"

"Yes, of course. I am tired."

"You aren't just saying this so you can leave our date?"

"I am not."

"Because I don't want to run into you later tonight at a
bar or anything. That would be awkward."

"It would, but it won't happen. I can promise you that."

"Fine, in that case I wish you a good night's rest. It's
been a pleasure, Tom."

She got up and left. I think she was offended,
but I couldn't blame her. She had wanted to see me for
quite some time and I had kept putting it off. Like I said,
there was nothing wrong with her, but I just didn't feel
like I wanted to put any effort into conquering her.
She just didn't do it for me. It was as simple as that.

I waited for our server to return, settled the bill and
began the walk home. It wasn't a long walk, and the
summer air provided a nice opportunity to clear my head.

I reached the canal locks and paused at the bridge.
Looking north, I could see the quiet across the river.
Turning around and facing south, I could see the quiet
here. There wasn't much going on that night.
Though, to be fair, there rarely is much going on any
night. Sure, on a weekend, there is always a small
concentrated fury of excitement on Elgin and another in
the Byward, but on the whole, it was a sleepy city. I had
grown sleepy with it and spent much of my time drifting
in and out. There wasn't much else for me to do. I could
hold my hands up to the sky and wait for a chariot to
appear in the clouds and take me away, but I'm sure my
arms would grow weary long before that were to happen.

I avoided walking down Elgin, not because of the noise
or the riff-raff, but for fear of running into Celeste.
I wasn't planning on going to a bar, but I didn't want her
to see me and assume that I was on my way to one.
After the city hall, I turned down a side street and made
my way back to the canal. I had done a bit of a detour,
but that was mostly to avoid Confederation Park at night.
I have no special desire to be stabbed tonight, not by
needle nor by knife. At the canal, I make my way down
to the path and slowly jaunt my way south. It's fairly
deserted, but I see a few souls out by the water. There is
a trio sharing a bottle of wine sitting on one of the
benches. They are far too old to be drinking illegally, but
such are the laws in this puritanical country that it's a
crime to drink in public. No, not like in those civilised
countries in Europe where it is completely appropriate to
sit in a park with a cold drink. Here we turn it into
contraband and turn innocent civilians into rogues. The
trio hardly look like trouble. I think one of them was
wearing a tie. They probably went to unwind after work
and kept rolling with it. I can't blame them. It's a lovely
summer's night, even if it's a bit quiet.

I reach my street and turn away from the canal. Another
time, dear friend, I think to myself. There aren't many
notable topographic features in this city to take the
breath away, but I'll always have time for the ditch that
Colonel By dug. It is charming under lamp standards in

the summer's night and even better at winter, when it is
transformed into the world's longest skating rink.
I open the door to my brick townhouse and head straight
for the kitchen. I really could use a drink. Celeste has
taken a lot of effort out of me, though for the life of me,
I can't recall how. We didn't speak about too many
things, nor were any of the topics sore subjects for me.
I am just tired. Perhaps it was a poor decision to go out
after a day of work. I always am in a better mood when
I've had a light nap in the afternoon. I'm absolutely
charming on a Saturday when I can take a short rest.
I don't care if people consider naps for children and the
elderly; it is absolutely a delight. I wouldn't be opposed to
a culture that embraces the siesta. When a hot summer
day is wearing you down, why not take an hour or so
and recharge the batteries? It's far too late for a siesta
now. If I lay my head down it will be for good and I won't
be up until the morning. It's sometimes a struggle to
decide how long I should want to stay awake. As much
as I might be tired, there is still something nice about
being awake. Only then can I truly know that I am alive.
This is real. When I feel sluggish, it is okay, because
I can feel it.

Despite my best intentions at trying to stay awake,
I decide that for my body's sake I should go to sleep.
For what it was worth, I had promised Celeste that
I would be straight to bed. With a glass of single malt
whisky in hand, I headed upstairs. Walking past the
study, I decided to pause and grab a book. Nothing
really winds me down for sleep like reading a chapter
and sipping fine scotch. It sounds pretentious, perhaps,
but I won't let anyone tell me that those aren't two of the
best things a man could enjoy. I've got a few nice
collections of both. In my study, I've been collecting
enough books that it really could be a library.
Every Monday, I go to the bookstore and buy one book.
I never pay full price, always choosing something that is
on the discounted shelves. That is not to say that I don't
choose good books, it's just that I am selective about
when I am to buy a certain book. Having a vast
collection built over the years, I'm not necessarily in

need of any particular book at any time, so I will wait
until a hardcover version of a classic or a recent critically
acclaimed novel or an anthology of poetry goes on sale.
I have little interest in trash, though I will pay bottom
dollar. Having said that, while I buy a book each week,
I rarely read as quickly as that. When I am blessed with
time, perhaps I will read an entire novel in a weekend.
Otherwise it might take weeks or even months.
Such is life, correct? And, when I am reading, it doesn't
hurt to accompany it with something that tickles the taste
buds. I've been interested in scotch since I was a young
boy. There was always a bit of mystery about it.
That's the thing, too, about scotch, is that the mystery
doesn't disappear when you grow up. It's still there.
To me it was always a drink that carried a weight. It
wasn't something that was thrown around or that you'd
see a lout on the street corner drinking. No, this was the
sort of thing that came out when a celebration was in
order. Toasts were given in the name of Lagavulin,
Glenmorangie, Glenfiddich, Glenlivet and Oban. This
was the nectar of the gods. Islay and Speyside were
Olympus. Grandpa would sit you on his lap and let you
smell the mystic drink in his hand. As a grown man,
I still pour myself two fingers of scotch over two ice
cubes, because that's the way my Pa would take it.
I won't mess with tradition.

I grab a book off the shelf and head into my bedroom.
It's a bit messy, but that's okay, right, because a man's
bedroom is his inner sanctum. This is holy ground and
only the most worthy are to enter. I set the scotch on the
nightstand and the book on the bed. In my dresser I find
my pyjamas. I don't know if I am to feel dignified or silly
as a grown man in pyjamas. I've been wearing them for
years, but I still don't know the answer to that. Crawling
into bed, I take the book and begin to read. The scotch
warms my lips in the most pleasant way. I've chosen a
bit of Isle of Jura to enjoy tonight. It's nothing special,
but it is a simple delight.

I don't know when I fell asleep, but I remember waking
up. There was a loud noise outside my house.

It sounded like a car crash or some other clashing of metal. I rushed to the window to see. Outside there was nothing at all. The street was empty and I couldn't see if it was just a skunk or a raccoon messing with someone's garbage cans. Absolutely nothing, turning away from the window I looked back at my bed and there, out of nowhere appeared a Spirit. My face turned pale (I imagine, though I couldn't see myself).
With a trembling mouth I tried to form words.

"Wh-wh-wh-what do you want with me?"

The Spirit, who was clothed in a three-piece suit and a bowler cap, just smiled back at me.

"P-p-please. I don't understand who or what you are. What are you doing here? Why have you come to me?"

The Spirit looked at me and tipped his cap. I saw a bright flash of light and closed my eyes to protect them.
When I could sense that it was no longer bright out (the way one's eyes can tell), I opened my eyes to see that I was looking down from a very high vantage point. Way below me I could see a busy intersection and cars that looked miniscule to me.

"Where am I?"

The Spirit laid his hand on my shoulder, it seemed as if to comfort me, and then finally spoke.

"You ought to ask first, when you are."

"Okay, when and where am I, strange Spirit? And, also, who are you?"

"You are back on May 17th, 2002."

"Wait, that's my birthday!"

"Yes."

"It was my twenty-first birthday. I remember now. I know where I am. This is Barcelona below."

"Si."

I turn around and look at the highly detailed tower.

"You've brought me to la Sagrada Familia."

"Yes."

"But why? And, who are you?"

"I've come to show you a few things."

"Wait, are you the Ghost of Christmas Past or something?"

"No, of course not. It's May."

"The Ghost of Birthdays Past?"

"No, it's just a coincidence that this happens to have been on a birthday. It's not like I can only show you birthdays or anything. I'm not even a ghost, really."

"What are you?"

"I'm a figment of your imagination, Tom Armstrong."

"So this is all just made up?"

"Yeah, pretty much."

"But why?"

"The mind is a complex organ, Tom. I can't explain half the things that it does and that's only counting the ten percent that you use."

"Am I dreaming then?"

"Call it what you like, Tom. It's yours in any case."

"Why am I here, in the past? Is that not a dream?"

"Some people call them memories."

"What do I have to remember about something a decade ago?"

"You were young. You were happy. You were in love."

"Of course. Barcelona. Bridget."

"You brought her here on vacation."

"Yes, I wanted to take her to Spain for a holiday. It was going to be the first trip that we ever took together. We had been dating for maybe a year. I remember. Wait, you've brought me back to that trip on my birthday? Why did you do that?"

"I'm only a figment of your imagination, Tom. Remember? Why have I brought you here? What happened?"

Another flashing light crosses my eyes and I hold up my arm to shield them. When the light passes, I lower my arm to see a sidewalk café.

"Las Ramblas."

Seated at a table, maybe thirty feet away was me, only a lot younger. He was skinnier and smiled more. Across from him sat Bridget, my girlfriend at the time. We are too far away to hear what they are saying, but I know exactly what conversation it was. Bridget and I had been dating for about a year and on three different occasions she had thought that I was going to propose to her. I had told her I loved her many times and I suppose she thought that I was planning to marry her. The first time she thought that I was going to ask her to marry me was about six months in to our relationship. It was New Year's Eve and we had gone to the ballet and an expensive dinner downtown. There was a party that one of her friends had and I took her to it. Just before midnight, I asked her if she would mind sneaking away from the crowd into the back garden.

I don't know why she expected something more,
but when we got to the back garden, I asked her if she
wanted to have sex at the drop of the clock. I thought it
would be really cool to ring in the New Year by having
sex. I was twenty, okay? Except, before I could finish
asking the question, she was shouting with glee that yes,
she would marry me. Then she heard the rest of my
question. Needless to say she was very disappointed
and suffice it to say we did not begin 2002 on the best of
terms. The second time she thought I was going to ask
her was on my birthday, in Barcelona.

"I don't want to watch this. Take me away."

"You're in control, Tom. Take yourself away."

"You're a lousy figment, you know that."

"These are your memories, this is your mind.
Choose somewhere else to be."

"I can't now. I've already started thinking about that
moment. I can't help but watch it over again."

I stood there and saw my younger self cause that poor
girl to cry. She stood up and she ran away. I sat there
and didn't know what to do. Expectations are terrible
things. I'm just glad that my mind didn't bring us to the
third time Bridget thought I was going to propose.
I'll share it with you, anyways. It was October that year,
Thanksgiving weekend. We had been struggling as
a long distance couple for about six weeks, as she was
in one city finishing her last year of undergrad and I was
in another starting my graduate program.
Every two weeks one of us had gone to visit the other.
It sounds like a lot, but in reality it meant that at that
Thanksgiving we had maybe seen each other ten days
total since the summer, when we had spent nearly every
day together. We were sitting outside; it was actually
nice for a change in October, and looking at the stars.
We started talking about things and how they were
going. I think Bridget was waiting for me to make some

reassuring statement. I began to speak, and I can't remember the exact words I used, but I told her that it just couldn't work any longer. She didn't run away that time, but she sat there and cried. She told me that she had been looking at houses for the following summer near my university. She said that she had thought that we were going to get married when she finished school. I didn't know what to say. It's hard when one person is looking far ahead and they can see the light at the end of the tunnel while the other person isn't so sure there is light or just an oncoming train. I don't know if I panicked because I might have thought about the possibility (she had already thought that I was going to propose twice before) or something else. I just needed out. Over the next couple of weeks we made sure each of us got back our stuff and I think she called me on Christmas, but I wasn't home and I didn't return the call. That was the last I heard of Bridget. Until now.

I stand watching my younger me sit clueless on the sidewalk café. He'd agonise that poor girl for another six months, and who knows how long after. But there was nothing I could do to intervene. This wasn't time travel. This was just a memory.

**

"Let's go somewhere else, now, okay?"

The Spirit put his hand on my shoulder and I saw the bright light begin again. I closed my eyes and could feel the warmth of the sun on my face. It became comfortable again and I opened my eyes.

I am seated at a desk. I stare at the Spirit with venomous eyes. I can't believe that he has done this to me. Of all the supernatural beings to visit, I had to have him.

My mind softens as I remember that he has already
announced that he isn't really a spirit, but a figment of
my imagination.

"Why are we here?"

"You've brought us here, Tom."

"I didn't ask where we were, Spirit, I asked why.
Why have you, I mean, why have I brought us here?"

A woman in a pencil skirt and tight red blouse walks by.
She is in a rush and doesn't stop to say hi.
This is strange to me, because upon further observation,
it is quite clear to me that the woman is Celeste.
She always made a habit of stopping to say a few words.
It had become a bit clingy, but I think the affection
overruled the annoyance.

"Why didn't she stop, Spirit?"

"I don't know, Tom. Does she usually?"

"You're an awful thing, you know that? You know
perfectly well, if you are a figment of my imagination,
that Celeste always stops to say hello."

"Did it bother you?"

"What do you mean?"

"Did it bother you when she stopped?"

"Yes. Well, not always. I knew that she liked me.
It was nice to have the attention."

"It's not nice being ignored, is it?"

"Are you going to turn this into some sort of moralizing
story, Spirit?"

"No."

"You aren't?"

"No, I have no intention of teaching you anything.
I am just a figment, remember?"

"I feel like I've been Dickensed. I am expecting this to be
the bloody Ghost of the Present or something."

"Does this look like the present-day to you?"

"Yes, it's identical to the way the office looked today.
Celeste is even wearing the same outfit."

"Well then I guess it is the present."

"You are awful, Spirit."

"I'm a figment."

"I'll prefer to call you Spirit, thanks."

I stand up from my desk and walk around the office.
It becomes clear from the fact that nobody notices me
that I don't really exist to them. Or, perhaps, more
accurately, they don't exist. This is my imagination,
after all.

"Spirit, I can't interact with them, can I?"

"I don't know. Do you want to?"

I wasn't sure. I liked the thought of being a bit of a
voyeur to see what they thought of me when I wasn't
around, but then I remembered that this being my
imagination, I'd only be observing what I thought they
might think of me. It was less gratifying than I thought.

"No, it's fine. It doesn't matter."

Out of the corner of my eye, I saw Celeste, only this time
I finally saw her for what she was. She was standing at
the water cooler, filling up her recyclable aluminium
bottle when her face went crooked. She was frowning. I
don't know what it was about that frown, but it caught
me. She then put the aluminium bottle down and began
inspecting the taps to the water cooler. No more water

came out. She lifted the empty jug off the top and put it down beside the cooler. Next to the cooler was a stand of full jugs. Without hesitation, Celeste picked up one, pulled the plastic tab off the cap and dumped the thing back into the water cooler. No issues, she pulled it off without a hitch. She then picked up her aluminium bottle and continued to fill it. She drank a bit of water, topped off the bottle and walked away. She was incredible.

"Did you see that, Spirit?"

"Oh, that, yeah, that Celeste is something else, isn't she?"

"She is!"

"It's too bad you blew your chance."

"What?"

"You only ever got that one date with her."

"I was tired! I'm sure she would understand."

"How long had she been waiting for that one date?"

"I don't know."

"Think long and hard, Tom."

"Good God, she had been flirting with me for ages. Did I really blow it?"

"Yes, I can assure you, you'll never have another chance with her."

"For a figment of my imagination, you sure have certitude about you."

"I just know things. Things you might not have noticed."

**

"This is my bedroom."

"You are really good at this game, Tom."

"What have I to see here?"

"The end."

"I don't understand."

"There is no third act for you, Tom."

"I don't understand."

"What have I shown you so far?"

"I thought I had been showing myself?"

"Sure, semantics, Tom. What have you shown yourself so far?"

"Well, we went back a decade to Barcelona and Bridget and to the present and Celeste. So, like I said, I feel like I've been Dickensed and you've shown me the past and present and now you're going to show me the future. It's at that point that I'll be scared and change my ways and be a better person, right?"

The Spirit stared at me.

"Right?"

The Spirit, or figment of my imagination as I had been told he was just stared at me. I didn't know what to do. How do you command a non-entity to respond? I looked back at the Spirit, hoping that he'd finally speak. I felt my pyjamas go cold and looked over at the window and could see that it was open.

"There is no third act, Tom."

Everything went black and I felt nothingness. It was the
most excruciating feeling I had ever experienced.
Every piece of me that had a beat was gone and
my entire soul vacated. I not only felt nothing,
I was nothing. I became nothing. I returned to nothing.
There would be no third act. I am the dust.

Acknowledgements

None of this would have been possible without the continued support of my "real world job" employers. I thank them for giving me the opportunity to slip out the back for a couple of months and indulge myself in galleries, beers and prose.

I also want to thank my family for their tremendous support of who I am and what I attempt to do. It means the world to me that they are always behind me.

Specifically, I must thank/blame my parents for infecting me with the travel bug. It's their fault that I want to explore the world out there.

www.ingramcontent.com/pod-product-compliance
Lightning Source LLC
Chambersburg PA
CBHW050427260626
47156CB00003B/1191